Tito's Dedication

To my wife Margaret and my children Ronny, Audrey and Tito Puente Jr.

Jim's Dedication

To my nephew, the late Samuel Giles Payne VI, a music lover and musician of exceptional talent, whose difficult struggle with schizophrenia has inspired many people.

Publisher's Note

From the original publication, "*Tito Puente's Drumming with the Mambo King*" (2000, Hudson Music)

In the final days of working on this book ("Drumming with the Mambo King"), the sad news came that Tito Puente had passed away. We had been working with the maestro for almost two years, preparing this manuscript and DVD. The content is being presented exactly as Tito last saw it. Nothing has been changed. Tito was very excited about its completion and greatly looking forward to its release. We feel privileged to have worked with him and we dedicate this project to the Mambo King, a man of great humanity, spirit, wisdom, music and humor.

—*Rob Wallis and Paul Siegel / Hudson Music*

Tito Puente - King Of Latin Music
by Jim Payne
ISBN#: 1423413350
Catalog#: 331438

Visit Hudson Music online at
www.hudsonmusic.com

◆

Executive Producers
Rob Wallis and Paul Siegel
◆

Tito Puente Curator, Music Historian and Archival Photographs
Joe Conzo
◆

Filmed at Daily Planet Studios, Creskill, New Jersey
& at Tito Puente's Restaurant, City Island, New York
◆

Editing
Michael Lydon
◆

Additional Editing
Ed Uribe
◆

Cover Design & New Layout
Jo Hay
◆

Book Design, Image Editing, Music Engraving
Dancing Planet MediaWorks™
◆

DVD Production and Editing
Phil Fallo & Jim Payne
◆

Photography
**Eleonora Alberto (inside photos where noted),
Martin Cohen (inside photos where noted - www.congahead.com),
Joe Conzo, Jr. (inside where noted), Bruce Klauber (additional photos for DVD)**
◆

Special thanks to MARGIE PUENTE, DR. BRUCE KLAUBER
◆

Proofreading
Rick Szykowny, Harry Weinger

Tito Puente: 1923 - 2000
Tribute to a King - By Jim Payne

Tito Puente, the King of Latin Music, passed away on May 31, 2000, at age 77. He was arguably the most important Latin musician of the last 50 years. I had the privilege of collaborating with him on several projects. He was an inspiration to me and I can truly say that he was a remarkable person in every respect. His energy, humor and good-time spirit will be deeply missed by me and his millions of fans throughout the world.

For drummers, Tito Puente was to the timbales what Buddy Rich and Tony Williams were to jazz drums. He was the undisputed King of the Timbales, the "fastest gun in the west." He combined the snare drum and drumset techniques of Western music with the traditional Cuban style, and with innovation and hard work, he took performance on the timbales to a new level. He brought the timbales out in front of the band, played them standing up and made them a featured instrument, much the way Gene Krupa had done with the drumset. Latin music authority José Rizo has called his experimental, all-percussion album, *Puente In Percussion*, "the most incredible recorded percussion session in history."

Tito was a master musician, proficient on piano, vibes, saxophone and drumset as well as timbales, and he was also a charismatic entertainer. As soon as he walked on stage, the party began. Santana knew, when he recorded a version of the 1963 Tito Puente recording, "Oye Como Va," that he was borrowing from a master composer, whose carefully constructed compositions, rooted in percussion, were guaranteed to create an irresistible dance groove.

Tito Puente, "El Rey Del Timbal," ca. 1951. The Palladium Ballroom.

Table of Contents.

Photo by Eleonora Alberto

Tito in 2000.

Tito's Note

Photo by Eleonora Alberto

As a musician my work has denied me. I've spent lonesome holidays away from my family and lost many hours of sunshine. But I do not regret it because an artist must do what he feels... it was something I felt I had to do. If my music has brought joy to one person, then I have been successful.

This book and DVD contain a great deal of information about my life, my music and my style of playing, as well as a short history of the music which has been my life's work.

Stay on the clave, and good luck.

Tito Puente

Jim's Note

Photo by Marilynne Herbert

Ever since I heard the bass from the Latin social club coming through the wall of my East Village basement apartment and bought *Puente In Percussion* from the Times Square Record Shop in the 42nd St. subway station, I've been hooked on Latin music.

This project has been very exciting for me. Working with Tito Puente has been a great privilege and I've learned a lot. I'm very thankful to him, especially, and also to Brian Theobold, Ina Dittke, Paul Siegel, Rob Wallis, Joe Conzo, Michael Lydon, José Madera, Louis Bauzó, Ed Uribe and Joanna Fitzpatrick.

Kim Payne

About Jim Payne.

Jim Payne has played drums with the J.B. Horns, Mary Wells, Esther Phillips, the Blues Magoos, Hank Ballard & the Midnighters, the Radio City Orchestra, Chuck Rainey, Mike Brecker, Slickaphonics and his own band, The Jim Payne Band. He studied drums with Jim Strassburg, Sonny Igoe, Henry Adler, Philly Joe Jones, Bernard Purdie, José Madera and Johnny Almendra. He has a BA from Yale University, an MBA from Columbia University and has attended the Manhattan School of Music.

He has taught drums for many years, authored *Funk Drumming, The Complete Book of Funk Drumming, Drums From Day One* and *The Great Drummers of R&B, Funk & Soul* for Mel Bay Publications.

Payne has also produced records for Medeski, Martin & Wood, the J.B. Horns, Alfred "Pee Wee" Ellis, Fred Wesley, Yvonne Jackson, Mike Clark/Paul Jackson and his own band, The Jim Payne Band.

Jim welcomes you to contact him directly:
Web Page: www.funkydrummer.com
E-mail: jpayne@funkydrummer.com

About the Photos.
and the Discography

Photo by Joe Conzo, Jr.

The majority of the photos were supplied from the private collection of Joe Conzo. Joe, who also helped with the discography, is a music historian and archivist specializing in Tito Puente. He worked with Tito for many years and contributed much valuable information about Tito's life and recorded work for this book.

Tito in 1965.

Tito Puente

King of Latin Music

*"There is a rose in Spanish Harlem,
A red rose up in Spanish Harlem..."**

W HEN YOU CUT THROUGH THE ROMANCE AND GET INTO THE STREETS, SPANISH HARLEM, THE LEGENDARY BIRTHPLACE OF AFRO-CUBAN MUSIC IN NORTH AMERICA, IS NOT THAT BIG AND IT'S NOT THAT BEAUTIFUL. A LONG NARROW SLICE OF MANHATTAN, "EL BARRIO" OR THE DISTRICT, AS RESIDENTS CALL IT, LIES SQUEEZED EAST-TO-WEST BETWEEN 3RD AND 5TH AVENUES AND STRETCHES FROM BLACK HARLEM'S FAMOUS 125TH STREET SOUTH TO 96TH STREET, WHERE THE ELEGANT UPPER EAST SIDE BEGINS. A high, blackened stone wall, the track-bed of the Harlem and New Haven Railroad, bisects the neighborhood, and pedestrians have to walk through dank, narrow tunnels to pass from one side to the other. It's a checkerboard neighborhood, blocks of weather-beaten apartment buildings, five- and six-story walkups, interspersed with weedy vacant lots. Steel gates to keep out burglars cover the apartment windows, and every night shopkeepers roll down ribbed metal armor over their storefronts and secure it with heavy-duty padlocks. Trash cans overflow onto the streets and sidewalks.

The "Barrio" of Spanish Harlem vibrates with rich traditions and down-to-earth culture. The smell of fried plantains and rice and beans drifts out into the streets from red- and yellow-fronted bodegas and delicatessens. The sweet-hot sounds of Latin music fill the air from speakers in front of mom-and-pop record stores and from car radios. In the summer, girls chalk hopscotch squares on the sidewalks, and boys play stickball games between parked cars. Housewives lean out of first-floor windows to chat with friends, while old men sit on folding chairs by worn stone stoops and play cards and dominos. The avenues teem with traffic, and the honking horns and the rumble of the subway coming up through the pavement announce that El Barrio is in one of the world's largest cities, New York, with its glittering skyscrapers and rushing crowds, a city where the best and the worst of everything, the haves and have-nots, exist side by side. In El Barrio it's easy to

*Lyrics from "Spanish Harlem," Ben E. King, 1961, writers: Jerry Leiber and Phil Spector.   9

see what you can get if you're lucky and where you could end up if you're not.

Tito Puente, recognized as the world's greatest timbale player and Latin music's best-loved goodwill ambassador, was born in Spanish Harlem and was educated in its schools and in its streets. Combining the musical heritage he learned there with his own

determination and energy, he became one of the most successful Latin bandleaders of all time. But whether he's playing at Carnegie Hall or a concert to benefit his scholarship fund for young musicians, Tito acknowledges his humble beginnings in El Barrio. If you're from El Barrio, you're proud of it. That's where you grew up and that's where you learned how to survive.

◆ ◆ ◆

In the early 1920s, a young couple from Puerto Rico, Ernest and Ercilia Puente, boarded a ship in San Juan and spent five days sailing to New York to begin a new life. Though they had heard of

Tito at age 3.

opportunities, they knew there would be obstacles. The language was different and the city was unfamiliar territory. They didn't know what to expect. The first wave of immigrants from the Caribbean islands, Cubans and Puerto Ricans ready and willing to take on the challenge of a new life, had gained a toehold in New York, but they had to fight for every inch of ground.

When the Puentes stepped off the ship they needed a place to live. Ernest also needed a place to work. Determined to make his way in this strange new environment, he finally landed a job in the Gem razor blade factory in Brooklyn. After a short stay in a Brooklyn apartment, they moved to Manhattan's East 110th St., joining other Spanish speakers in the neighborhood that became known as El Barrio. A conscientious worker, Ernest rode the subway to the factory every day and was soon promoted to foreman. At home, too, the young couple's dreams started to take shape. Ercilia gave birth to their first child. Their new son, Ernest Anthony Puente Jr., was born in Harlem Hospital on April 20, 1923. They called him Ernestito, and eventually everyone shortened that to Tito. He was the future King of Latin Music.

Early Years

It didn't take long for young Tito to gravitate toward his life's passion. As a toddler he began to use forks and spoons to bang on the furniture and window sills of their Spanish Harlem apartment. Instead of discouraging what many might consider a questionable pastime in the thin-walled, close quarters of a Barrio apartment building, Ernest and Ercilia encouraged their budding percussionist. Soon, however, the youthful banging coming from the Puente apartment began to disturb the other tenants. "I was a very percussive young man, always playing on things," Tito recalls with a chuckle. "My neighbors complained to my parents, 'Why don't you put that brat to *study* music? He's driving us crazy here!'"

To appease her neighbors Ercilia enrolled her boy in piano lessons at the New York School of Music on 125th and Lenox Ave. Tito's course of study had begun. He was eight years old. The lessons cost 25 cents and in those days a hard-working factory foreman may have considered that an unnecessary luxury. To avoid any possible opposition, Ercilia waited until Ernest Sr. was asleep before tiptoeing into the bedroom to take the money from his pants pockets.

As the dutiful young mother walked her son to the Music School on Lenox Ave., about twenty minutes away, the young boy's eyes and ears were bombarded by the sights and sounds of his buzzing neighborhood. The Park Plaza Ballroom was down the street at 110th and 5th Ave., the Golden Casino across the street on the same corner, and Club Cubanicán close by on the next block. Tito could hear popular Cuban and Puerto Rican songs of the day from open apartment windows and restaurants. Record shops attracted customers by letting music overflow into the street—one record shop on Madison Ave. between 113th and 114th was owned by Victoria Hernández, sister of one of Puerto Rico's most famous composers, guitarists and flute players, Rafael Hernández.

During the 1930s many of the Jewish theaters in Spanish Harlem changed their names and began catering to the neighborhood's growing Latin community. The Photoplay Theater became the San José, the Mount Morris at 116th and 5th became the Campoamor, and musicians began arriving from Cuba and Puerto Rico to play in the pit orchestras. Further west, Tito and his mother passed the famous Apollo Theater on 125th St., which featured the best black bands of the day—blues, gospel and jazz—as well as vaudeville shows.

In 1928 Ercilia gave birth to a baby girl, Anna, and when Anna was six and Tito eleven, their mother enrolled both children in dance school. Soon they were an amateur dance team. An old photo shows Tito at the age of twelve, standing very straight in black tails and white tie, holding seven-year-old Anna's hand in a formal dance position. "Annie and I studied all forms of ballroom dancing including acrobatic tap," Tito recalls. "We were inspired of course by Fred Astaire and Ginger Rogers. I pride myself on being one of the few band leaders who really knows how to dance."[1] Tito and Anna also joined a children's talent group in Spanish Harlem called the Stars of the Future, sponsored by their local Catholic Church, La Milagrosa. Anna was crowned Queen of the Stars of the Future in 1935, but her feisty young brother was not to be outdone. Tito was crowned King of the Stars of the Future four times. It seems the future King of Latin Music was getting used to that title early in his career.

A Teenager in El Barrio

Living in an ethnically diverse neighborhood can force young boys to grow up quickly, and Tito acquired his street smarts early on. "Around the neighborhood," Tito remembers, "one side we had the Italians, the other side we had the Blacks, and the Puerto Ricans were smack in the middle!" A regular boy, Tito loved to play games with the other kids, especially baseball. But whatever aspirations he may have had in sports and dancing were cut short by a serious bicycle accident which injured one of his ankles. From then on he concentrated on his music. After his early school years at Public School 43, Tito moved on to Cooper and then Galvani Junior High, where he began developing another music-related talent: singing. He joined a vocal quartet and sang songs by the Ink Spots and other popular groups of the day.

Meanwhile, in the larger world, the big bands were taking the country by storm. Swing dance music was on the radio and on the juke-boxes, and big bands played live in the hotels and the theaters of Times Square. Tito soaked it all in. "I would listen to the great dance bands of the day on the radio, Benny Goodman, Artie Shaw, Duke

Ellington, Count Basie and Chick Webb, and I'd go to theaters like the Paramount and the Strand to see them perform. My hero was Gene Krupa." In fact, Krupa inspired Tito to begin playing the drumset. After hearing his hero's famous floor tom solo on "Sing, Sing, Sing," Tito began playing trap drums. The drumset was really Tito's first percussion instrument, not the timbales. Eventually young Tito won $10 playing "Sing, Sing, Sing," note for note, in a kids' drumming contest.

On the other hand, the Latin music of his Afro-Cuban heritage also intensely interested Tito: Machito, Rafael Hernández, Noro Morales, Arsenio Rodríguez and Cuban pianist Anselmo Sacasas. Sacasas, eleven years older than Tito, had played with the Orquesta Casino de la Playa in Havana, and Tito was fascinated by his piano solo on Miguelito Valdés' "Dolor Cobarde." Listening to the music of these two different cultures greatly influenced the original music that Tito would write in later years.

Since he was listening to different styles of music, Tito went to different teachers to master the various techniques each style required. He continued his piano lessons with Victoria Hernández, Rafael Hernández' sister, and also studied with Luis Verona, the pianist with Machito's Afro-Cuban Orchestra. He was getting to know some of the best Cuban musicians on the New York Latin scene.

He also began drumset lessons with a man he remembers only as Mr. Williams. "Mr. Williams knew absolutely nothing about Latin music," says Tito, "but I wasn't going to him for that. He gave me a good foundation, snare drum technique, how to interpret figures in charts and to accompany shows." Tito knew that all the big band musicians had to read music and since playing in a big band was one of his goals, he religiously set about acquiring the skills he'd need.

First Gigs

By fifteen Tito had been studying piano and drums for seven years—some called him El Niño Prodigo (The Child Prodigy). Inquisitive and smart, Tito picked up things quickly. He began playing around the neighborhood with his friends at informal dances and church affairs, and sat in with other bands. He hung around the Park Plaza on 110th and 5th Ave. and began playing the drumset semi-professionally there on Sunday afternoons with a group called Federico Pagani's Happy Boys. Pagani's swing-oriented group was not a great orchestra, but the people liked them because they played the music of the time—pop, Latin, jazz, swing, a little of everything.[2]

With the Happy Boys, Tito began to apply the drumming techniques he had been studying to the instrument that made him famous: the timbales. Cuban-born José Montesino was the Happy Boys' timbalero, and the future El Rey de Timbal was eager to learn all he could from this seasoned professional.

Montesino willingly showed the young Puerto Rican authentic Cuban rhythms and techniques. Tito set up his timbales next to his drumset and began doing double duty as drummer and timbalero. "Everything I hear from Tito Puente is so Cuban," says Cuban musicologist Dr. Olavo Alén Rodríguez. "He can do it better than most of the Cubans. When a Puerto Rican musician decides to play Cuban music, he does it better than the Cubans! Tito Puente's way of playing pailas is so Cuban, so authentic."[3]

Latin pianist and bandleader Noro Morales.

Tito was excited to have a younger brother when his mother gave birth to her third child, Robert Anthony, but the joy the baby brought to the Puente family was short lived. At four, the young boy died in a tragic fall from a fire escape. The scars from such a loss never fully heal, but somehow life in El Barrio has to go on. Dealing with such a tragedy early in life may have helped Tito develop the iron will-power that it takes to excel in music or in any field that requires a similar commitment.

At sixteen, Tito landed his first paying gig, a one-night stand with the Noro Morales Orchestra* at the Stork Club. But it was hard to get gigs in New York because he was too young to get a union card from New York's Local 802. This didn't stop the enterprising young man. He went across the Hudson River, got a card in New Jersey, and continued to hang out at the New York union hall. A Cuban piano player he met on a union job became important to Tito's career. José Curbelo had just moved to New York in 1939 and had been playing with Xavier Cugat. Excited

*Morales was a Puerto Rican-born pianist, composer and arranger who came to New York in 1935, formed his own band and became quite successful. His brother, Humberto Morales, played timbales and wrote a classic book in 1954 with Henry Adler called *How to Play Latin American Rhythm Instruments*, which also included a section by Ubaldo (Uba) Nieto, the famous timbale player with the Machito Orchestra.

by his professional success, Tito was already starting to strut his stuff, and Curbelo was impressed. "I thought I had seen the best drummers in Cuba," he remembers, "until I saw Tito perform."

When Curbelo got an offer to play a three-month gig as a side man in the Telleria Society Orchestra at the Beach Club in Miami, he didn't hesitate to recommend Puente for the drum chair. When Tito got the call, he was attending Central Commercial High School, but this was a real job and a real opportunity—the call he had been waiting for. It was a difficult decision: to stay with the family who had encouraged him and nurtured him, or leave them and school and follow his dreams. The music business could be cutthroat, and the life of a musician difficult. This was a watershed moment. At sixteen Tito made up his mind. He dropped out of school and went on the road.

Tito on traps at age 16. COE at top of bandstand stands for Centro Obrero Español Club, 102nd and Madison Ave. Ramón Olivero and His Orchestra played there during the 1930s and '40s. Tito had three coconuts attached to the front of his drumset. His uncle helped him carry it around to his gigs.

On The Road~Moving Up

Tito and Curbelo roomed together in Miami and ended up becoming close friends. Tito looked up to the the older Curbelo, and Curbelo mentored the young drummer in music, bandleading, and in the ways of the music business. Curbelo later had his own successful band that Tito played in but, more importantly, when Curbelo disbanded his own group in 1957 and set up the Alpha Booking Agency, he became Tito's agent. He made sure that the Tito Puente Orchestra was always at the top of his artists' roster list. The relationship that started on that first gig in Miami became a long and fruitful one.

In the next two years Tito landed a series of gigs on the road and in New York with some of the most respected Latin bands of the day, bands in which he perfected his performing techniques and deepened his musical knowledge. When he returned to New York from the Miami gig, he again found a job at the Stork Club, this time with Johnny Rodríguez, the brother of Pablo "Tito"

Latin bandleader José Curbelo.

Rodríguez. Next he headed west to Chicago to play at the Colony Club with Anselmo Sacasas, the man whose piano solo he had so admired a few years earlier.

Again, Tito was in good company, and his ties to the musical heritage of Cuba became stronger and stronger. In 1940 Tito joined Noro Morales on a permanent basis. Morales performed in films and, as a member of the band, Tito went to Hollywood, but titles indicate that the films were probably not high art: *The Gay Ranchero, The Mexican Jumping Bean* and *Cuban Pete.*

By 1941, at age nineteen, Tito must have been a highly accomplished percussionist because José Curbelo's uncle, Fausto, recommended him for the drum chair in what many consider the premier Latin band of the time—Machito and His Afro-Cubans. A self-confident Tito matter-of-factly explains, "I sat in with the band and Machito hired me."

Machito (né Frank Grillo) had come from Havana to New York in 1937, the first authentic *sonero*, or ad-lib style Cuban vocalist, in the city. He worked with several established bands, including Xavier Cugat's, before opening at Manhattan's Club Conga on December 1940 with his own band in a partnership with Mario Bauzá.

Bauzá, who had come to New York from Havana in 1926, holds an important place in the history of Latin music. A trumpet and saxophone player, and an exceptionally talented composer, Bauzá was one of the originators of Latin jazz or Cubop, as it came to be called. Both he and Dizzy Gillespie played in Cab Calloway's trumpet section, and he composed what became the first Afro-Cuban jazz tune, "Tanga," at a rehearsal at the Park Plaza Ballroom

The José Curbelo Band. Tito is listed on the back as playing timbales but doesn't appear in the picture. Singer Tito Rodríguez is third from the right.

in 1940. Bauzá led Machito's band until 1975.

When Tito joined Machito, the older musicians targeted him with good-natured pranks. Unused to staying up late, he'd sometimes fall asleep on his drum chair during the later sets. The older musicians would then tie his leg to the side of the chair and when he woke up he'd be surprised to find himself strapped in. Tito played drumset and timbales with Machito, and when featured playing timbales, he played standing up in front of the band. Tito continued this now-standard style of playing the instrument when he formed his own band in order to give cues more easily, and he could even jump and dance while playing without losing a beat. "There's a step I used to do," he recalls jokingly, "which I still do, when I play that number—which I don't!"

Conga player Chino Pozo, cousin of Chano Pozo, the percussionist and composer who played with Dizzy Gillespie, later joined Tito in the Machito rhythm section. Machito was one of the first Latin big band leaders to make congas a permanent part of the band.

Drafted for World War II

Tito's job with the premier Latin band of the day lasted less than a year. After the bombing of Pearl Harbor on December 7, 1941, the United States entered World War II, and all able-bodied young men were required to serve their country. Tito received his draft notice and packed up for boot camp in Long Beach, Long Island, to serve as a Seaman First Class in the U. S. Navy. Stationed aboard the USS Santee, an aircraft carrier that sailed through the Panama Canal to escort merchant supply ships in the South Pacific, Tito loaded ammunition into the ship's guns through nine naval battles during his two-year tour of duty. He and his shipmates were bombed, strafed and even torpedoed.

Tito, kneeling on the right, with his alto, and the band on the U. S. Navy ship USS Santee.

During the long stretches of downtime, however, Tito kept busy on his music. He had studied alto saxophone in New York with a well-known teacher, Joe Allard, and when he found the drum chair in the ship's band already filled, he concentrated on alto. A friendly Navy aircraft pilot, who played tenor sax and had arranged for Charlie Spivak's big band, taught the young seaman the basics of arranging, and Tito began writing his own music. Later he became the band's chief arranger and bandleader. (To test one early chart, he sent it back home to Machito, who tried it out with his band.) Tito and the USS Santee band entertained the tired troops on the hangar deck in the evenings, playing his arrangements of pop tunes like "Sweet Georgia Brown," "How High The Moon" and "One O'Clock Jump."

Ernesto and Ercilia Puente were proud of their young son, but fate was not so kind to their other children. After losing Robert, they now had to face the death of their daughter Anna from meningitis. Tito was informed of the tragedy while at sea and was allowed to go home for the funeral, but soon returned to duty.

Back From the War

The war ended in 1945 and Tito, along with millions of other soldiers and sailors, returned home with an honorable discharge. He tried to pick up where he had left off, but it wasn't easy. Federal policy stated that servicemen should get their old jobs back when they returned from duty, but when Tito approached Machito, he found that Ubaldo Nieto was now the timbalero. Uba had a wife and five kids and needed the job himself. Tito understood the situation and began to look for work elsewhere.

Fortunately, Tito's years of study and freelance experience had given him the tools he needed to take over the drum chair in almost any band, and he soon landed another series of first-class gigs. After a stint with Frank Marti at the Copacabana, he joined his old partner José Curbelo, who by now had formed his own big band. "At that time the Latin bands were playing nightclubs downtown like the Conga and the Havana Madrid," Tito recalls. "You had to be a good musician because we played the shows too, not just dance music or barrio music like in Spanish Harlem. You had to play waltzes, tangos, sambas, boleros. That's how I developed my experience in reading and playing all types of music. In the studio too, man, you had to know how to read music. You went in and you stopped at the eighth bar and you started on the ninth. Most of the Latin percussion musicians didn't

Pupi Campo on a 1946 album cover.

read much music. They always depended on the ear. Your ear can only go so far. Really, you just have to learn your profession, your instrument. This is it. *You have to study.*"[4]

Tito's next gig was with Pupi Campo, another Cuban bandleader playing the same circuit as Curbelo. When they shared the bill at the Havana Madrid on 58th St. with Dean Martin and Jerry Lewis,

Campo joined in as the third member of the famous comedy team. Eventually Tito became Campo's contractor and musical director. Tito became friends with Campo's trumpeter, Jimmy Frisaura, who later spent more than 40 years as a member of Tito's own band. Puerto Rican piano player José Esteves Jr. joined Campo's band, and he and Tito collaborated on songs and arrangements. Esteves' penchant for combining standard pop tunes with Latin rhythm was considered crazy by some Latin musicians and earned him the nickname "Joe Loco." Joe, who had played with Machito, Noro Morales and Count Basie, and later joined Tito's band, had studied at New York University and was familiar with the Schillinger System of Music, an influential approach to music theory among musicians and composers at the time.

Always curious about any new musical concepts, Tito studied the Schillinger system as well as traditional theory, conducting and orchestration with Richard Bender at Manhattan's prestigious Juilliard School of Music. "Those Juilliard lessons were $15," Tito remembers, "very expensive. I used to pay $7.50 and the GI Bill paid the other $7.50. I was trying to learn how to write motion picture music. Schillinger's graphs and the permutation of melodies interested me, but I found that wasn't my main goal. I stopped studying there a couple of years later and developed my style by performing and playing. Everybody reads the same books. Everybody goes to school. Everybody studies. Everybody graduates and gets a big diploma. They go home and put it up on the wall, and they just stare at it all the time. Musicians, dentists, doctors, everybody, it's the same thing. But to really learn, you've got to go on and practice and gain experience by playing in front of an audience."[5]

By now, Tito had been a side man and an arranger for some of the best in the business—Machito, Curbelo, Campo and ex-boxer and auto mechanic Miguelito "Mr. Babalu" Valdés, to name a few. He had also begun playing vibraphone and composing; some of his early tunes, "Cuando Te Vea" and "Pilareña," both with lyrics by Machito, were recorded by Pupi Campo. Soon it would be time for Tito to make his move.

Palladium Mural: Partial identification-Upper left corner: Pupi Campo, with large maracas. To the right: Machito. Below Machito, dancer Marlyn Winter. Bottom center: José Curbelo. Above and to the right of Curbelo: Tito Puente. Above and to the right of Tito with Mexican hat and shoulder scarf: Killer Joe Piro. Upper right corner: Miguelito Valdés.

The Palladium Era

In the 1950s America fell in love with the mambo and the "Home of the Mambo" was the Palladium Ballroom at 53rd and Broadway. Formerly the Alma Dance Studio, a popular "dance academy" where men could buy tickets and dance with hostesses, the Palladium had been converted into a nightclub by owner Tommy Morton in 1946. "The Palladium decided to hire Machito, who was very popular and sold a lot of records," according to Max Salazar, Latin music journalist, historian and DJ. "Machito's musicians, under Mario Bauzá's leadership, could play all kinds of music for the dancers, and the band had a large following, but Machito's Jewish fans didn't frequent the new venue, so Mario Bauzá asked owner Tommy Morton, 'How do you feel about black people?' 'Look,' he said, 'I'm only interested in the color of green.'"[6]

They decided to see if they could bring down the Harlem blacks

Tito Puente, "El Rey Del Timbal," ca. 1951. The Palladium Ballroom.

and Latinos who usually went to the Savoy or the Park Place Ballroom. To promote the Latino dance, they hired the same Federico Pagani who had led the Happy Boys. Pagani started a Sunday promotion, calling it the Blen Blen Club, after Chano Pozo's song "Blen-Blen-Blen," and he gave away discount cards at subway stations and bus stops. On the first Sunday a mob was waiting in line by four o'clock in the afternoon. Six Latin bands were booked, among them Noro Morales, José Curbelo and the headliner, Machito. According to Salazar, "The six Latin bands brought in Latinos, blacks and whites, and the guy made more money that Sunday than he had done in the months since he had opened up."[7]

This was the beginning of an era. The Palladium became the home of Latin music and the home of the mambo until it closed in 1966.

Machito wasn't always available, and to keep the Blen Blen Club going the Palladium needed other top bands. Pagani, who knew Tito from the Happy Boys days, was sitting one afternoon in 1948 in the Embassy Club when Tito was working on a new tune and singing the melodies he wanted the trumpet and bass to play. Pagani was dumfounded. "The music was so arousing it made my blood turn cold," he recalls. "What was the name of that tune?" he asked. Tito replied that he hadn't named it yet. "Es un picadillo," he said, "it's a mishmash." "Look," said the excited Pagani, "I'm going to book you into the Palladium on a Sunday. Put together a pickup group and we'll call it the Picadilly Boys."[8] Tito's career as a band leader had begun.

Tito's First Band

Tito continued playing with Pupi Campo while the Picadilly Boys played Sundays at the Palladium, but the writing was on the wall. In March of 1949 he left Campo to start his own band, taking some of Campo's men with him. They rehearsed at Luis Varona's mother's studio on 116th near Park Ave. The Palladium pickup band, which had included Charlie Palmieri on piano, was paired down from ten to seven players: Jimmy Frisaura and Gabriel "Chini" González, trumpets; Luis Varona, piano; Manuel Patot, bass; Angel Rosa, vocals; Frankie Colón, conga; and Tito on timbales and vibes. The band debuted on July 4, 1949, at the El Patio Club at Atlantic Beach, Long Island, and the gig lasted until Labor Day. When they returned to New York, Tito added Tony DiRisi as third trumpet and Chino Pozo on bongos, giving the band the form of the more traditional Latin trumpet conjunto.

Local 802 musicians hung out at New York's LaSalle Cafeteria and there Chino Pozo introduced Tito to Cuban singer Vincentico Valdés. An exceptional vocalist two years younger than Tito, Valdés had sung with Cuba's Septeto Nacional and had come to New York in 1946. He eventually sat in with Tito at the Palladium and the tune he sang, "Tus Ojos," went over so well the band had to play it again.

The pieces of the puzzle were beginning to fall into place. Tito's dream of a life in the music world—the dream that seemed so risky and far away when he left El Barrio and Central Commercial High for his first road gig—was coming true. He had paid his dues with some of the best and now he was leading his own band. All he needed next was a hit record.

Tito made his first recordings, including his first hit "Abaniquito," for the Tico label circa 1948-49. The Tico label, founded by George Goldner, was recording the New York Latin Bands. (Later, Goldner's Gee label became the home of Frankie Lymon & the Teenagers and other New York doo-wop groups.) (Tito later left Tico to join RCA for a short stint from 1949-51. During this time he recorded the original "Ran Kan Kan" and "Picadillo" 78s. He left RCA and rejoined Tico circa 1951.)

Mambos album cover, including the single "Abaniquito."

At his first Tico recording session in late 1948 at WOR studios on 48th St. and 7th Ave., Tito wanted to try something different with the augmented band, which included Mario Bauzá and Graciela (Machito's sister). "After recording three other tunes, Tito surprised us by passing out his charts for 'Abaniquito,' and dismissing the trombones and saxophones," remembers Frankie Colón, the conga player on the session. "The remaining musicians were Chino Pozo, Varona on piano, the four trumpeters, Frisaura, Di Risi, González, and Mario Bauzá, vocalists Graciela, Vincentico Valdés, and me. Vincentico was outta-sight ad-libbing and Mario blew his ass off on the solo."[9] After they listened back, Tito wanted to do it again, but Mario convinced him not to, insisting another take wouldn't come out as fiery.

Bingo, the hit record. Goldner had hired disc jockey Dick "Ricardo" Sugar to play Tico recordings nightly on a fifteen-minute radio program in New York. Sugar featured "Abaniquito" and, recalls Salazar, "The people went nuts. They went looking for the band and its records, asking, 'Who is this guy Tito Puente?' That's how it started."

Tito was off and running as a bandleader. First stop: the "cuchifrito circuit," the smaller venues that provided bread and butter for struggling Latin musicians. "Over the years I've earned my livelihood from the 'cuchifrito circuit,' and I made my name in it," Tito recalls. "It's been good to me and I can't put it down. If there were no 'cuchifrito circuit' I know a lot of bands that wouldn't be working today." The pay was low and the hours were long (many gigs lasted until 4 AM or later), but it was a start.

Tito's plan was simple. Step one: begin with a dedicated group of excellent musicians, "the boys," as he affectionately calls them. Tito insists on first-rate musicianship and he can be stern when he doesn't get it, but he also respects his fellow musicians and knows how to make them feel at ease. In 1951 Mongo Santamaria joined the band, replacing Frankie Colón on congas. Mongo left Cuba in 1949 and had played with Perez Prado before joining Tito. Charlie Palmieri came on board, replacing Gil Lopez on piano. (Gilberto Lopez had played piano from 1949-51 then left for the Korean War. He rejoined Tito in 1957 and remained with him for 17 years, for a total of 19 years and 11 months with Tito's band.) Charlie, older brother to Eddie Palmieri, was born in New York in 1927 of Puerto Rican parents and went on to become one of the most influential piano players on the Latin music scene. "The boys" were becoming a very strong group.

Step two: play high-quality dance music that satisfies your audience every time, and work, work, work until you increase the size of that audience and build up your marquee value. "Downtown we had the Palladium and the Arcadia," Tito remembers. "Uptown we had the Plaza, and in the Bronx we had ballrooms. The hotels gave a lot of Latin dances because they have beautiful ballrooms. We used to play all the resorts up in the Catskills, all the big hotels and out in the beach clubs in Long Island." The band also played gigs in New York, Los Angeles, Miami and Philadelphia.

On stage, Tito's energetic and charismatic personality began to emerge. "Nobody's got more energy than TP," says pianist Hilton Ruiz. Charlie Palmieri adds, "He's hard to keep up with, even walking down the street." Everyone liked the young bandleader as soon as he stepped on the bandstand. People identified with his enthusiasm and joined in the fun he seemed to be having on stage. He entertained them with good music and made them dance and forget the trials and tribulations of everyday life.

Tito's first album, *Tito Puente and Friends,* a compilation of 78s on a 10-inch 33 rpm disc, was released in 1951 on the Tropical label. The next year he recorded an incredible 37 singles for Tico. All he had to do was call up George Goldner and say he had something new, and Goldner would let him record it the next day. Cuban composers also sent him songs, and Tito put his arranging skills to work to give the tunes added appeal for American audiences.

The Mambo

As Tito was perfecting his sound and getting more recognition, the mambo was becoming more and more popular. The mambo featured medium to up-tempo, syncopated rhythms and horn lines; a strong tumbaó, or underlying rhythmic foundation, from the congas and the bass; and an infectious, syncopated guajeo, or repeated figure, from the piano. The sum: an intense and driving music perfectly suited for dancing. When the mambo came to New

Tito at the Palladium with his Leedy & Ludwig timbales.

York in the 1950s, via Perez Prado, Israel "Cachao" Lopez and Arsenio Rodríguez, it meshed perfectly with the new big band instrumentation of the Latin bands—four trumpets, four saxophones, four trombones and rhythm section. Combine the mambo with this powerful instrumentation and the arranging and bandleading skills of musicians like Mario Bauzá, René Hernández and Tito Puente, and you have a national dance

One of Tito's mambo albums for Tico, a compilation of 78 rpm singles.

craze. Although Prado's hits, "Mambo Jumbo," "Patricia" and "Cherry Pink and Apple Blossom White," probably introduced more Americans to Latin music, Tito's raw, high-energy, New York-style mambo was more authentically Cuban, more infectiously swinging and irresistible to dancers.

In 1952 the Palladium instituted an all-mambo policy featuring the best Latin bands. Who turned out to be Tito's biggest rival to take the title of "King of the Mambo" from Prado but Tito Rodríguez, a handsome singer who had been TP's boyhood friend, living only a few doors down the street in Spanish Harlem! A rivalry grew up between the two Titos, and at one point they even refused to announce each other as they traded sets on the Palladium bandstand. Puente was relentless in adding new material to his show and he stayed one step ahead. In the long run, however, the much-talked-about rivalry served another purpose, well understood by both competitors. As Tito Rodríguez said years later, "Rivalry is good for business."[10]

Business was booming, and night after night excited crowds climbed to the second floor of the building at 53rd and Broadway and packed the Palladium ballroom. According to Johnny Pacheco, "There were so many people moving at the same time in the Palladium that the floor used to shake. They had to reinforce it with steel beams to keep it from falling down. Everybody was going crazy." Marlon Brando sat in on bongos and Kim Novak and other movie stars created a stir at this celebrity hot spot.

New York nightlife columnist Pete Hamill painted a colorful picture of the Palladium in its heyday:

The Palladium was a girl in a shimmering black dress and high spiked heels, her glossy hair tossing to the rumble of mambo.

It was a dude in maroon pants with a 13 peg and a 44-inch knee dancing in a six-inch square with his hair slicked back in a DA, drowned in Kreml.

It was a bad guy from the Turbans or the Dragons wearing a Mr. B. collar and a one-button roll being dropped down the concrete steps by the bouncers and coming back with the boys in a fruit truck.

It was "Killer Joe" Piro teaching the pachanga to the swells; it was the guy who was found hanging by his fingers from a drainpipe one summer dawn, because he's fallen asleep in the men's room; it was Max Hyman, the nervous owner; it was the Brooklyn crowd in the leather seats, and the uptown crowd at the tables on the other side. Most of all it was Tito Puente and Machito and Tito Rodríguez. They made it into the greatest, baddest, most exciting dance hall of its time.[11]

With the excitement there came an interesting side effect. The Palladium was succeeding in an arena where governments and many learned professionals had not: race relations. The people who flocked there to dance the mambo came from all different ethnic backgrounds, African-American, Latino, Italian, Jewish and Irish. Race was simply not a consideration, and because of this, racial relations improved. "What social scientists couldn't do on purpose," says Salazar, "the mambo was able to accomplish by error."

Cubop and Birdland

During the Palladium era, Tito played a major role in the cross-fertilization of jazz and Latin music that became known as Cubop. "I combine the melodic concepts and harmonic changes of jazz," he says, "with the Latin percussion rhythms, without losing either's authenticity. Like Dizzy said, it's a marriage." Birdland, a basement club down the block from the Palladium, on the East side of Broadway between 52nd and 53rd, was a major center of the jazz scene. Originally called the Clique, Birdland was renamed after Charlie "Bird" Parker. It opened in 1949, with a 75 cent admission charge. Harry Belafonte was the first artist to play the new venue. All the bebop giants played at Birdland: Parker, Dizzy Gillespie, Max Roach and Thelonius Monk, to name a few. Latin musicians walked around the corner from the Palladium on their breaks to check out the Birdland scene, and jazz musicians like Stan Getz and Dexter Gordon walked over to the Palladium to check out "The Big Three": Machito, Tito Rodríguez and Tito Puente. TP was booked at Birdland, and alternated sets with John Coltrane, Art Blakey, Charlie Parker and Miles Davis.

Tito felt right at home in Cubop, but he never lost the beat and he never forgot about the dancers, the mainstay of his following. New York's radio listening audience fell in love with Tito when they heard his classic tunes, "Ran Kan Kan," "Barbarabatiri" and "Mambo Inn," broadcast live from Birdland dates MC'd by the gravel-voiced discjockey, Symphony Sid. In the "King of the Mambo" rivalry, it looked like TP would be the winner.

The Vibes

Somehow during this excitement, the hardworking bandleader managed to master the vibes and add them to his orchestra. "I was one of the first Latinos to play vibes with a Latin band," Tito

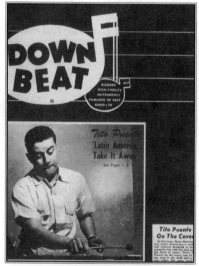

recalls. "I played them up at the Palladium. Cal Tjader used to come up when he was playing drums with George Shearing at Birdland, and that's where he got his idea to put the vibes into the George Shearing Quintet. A lot of people like my vibe playing, but some don't because they know me for my percussion work, the timbales. I couldn't be the King of everything, you know! The vibes are a difficult instrument to play. It takes knowing your keyboard harmonies, your changes, knowing the way to hit the notes to express your feelings. When I was at the Palladium, Latin people used to see me with the vibes and they'd say, 'Oh, here comes Tito with those venetian blinds again!' But those venetian blinds became very, very popular throughout the years."

Tito playing the vibes on the cover of Down Beat magazine.

Personnel Changes

Vincentico Valdés (who had recorded "Babalu" in 1941 with Xavier Cugat, years before Desi Arnaz) became Tito's lead singer and a key member of his organization until he received top billing over TP on a West Coast date. Having spent time in Mexico, Valdés had a large following there and in LA's Mexican-American community. The confusion provoked a rift between the singer and the bandleader, and Valdés left the band in 1953 when they returned to New York.

The two still remained friends, and Tito later wrote several arrangements for Vincentico when he went on his own, but by the end of 1953 he had hired Puerto Rican singer Gilberto Monroig. For three years after Monroig left the band in 1954, Tito worked without a lead singer. Always confident of his talent and his sound, he even boasted that his instrumental cha-chas didn't need vocals. (Like McDonald's fries don't need catsup!) He sang "coro" (chorus) himself, along with other members of the band, and he was starting to become more interested in jazz and percussion.

Another fiery drummer was making a name for himself on the New York scene: William Correa, nicknamed "Willie Bobo" by jazz pianist Mary Lou Williams. Born in Puerto Rico and raised in Spanish Harlem, Willie Bobo studied congas and timbales with Mongo Santamaria and Armando Peraza (who had come over from Cuba with Mongo in 1950), then began his career as Machito's band-boy. On Mongo's recommendation, Tito hired Bobo to replace Manny Oquendo on bongos, when Manny left the band.

Drums Only

With Willie Bobo, Mongo and himself, Tito had assembled what many consider his best rhythm section ever, one that recorded some of Tito's most adventurous percussion music. For *Puente In Percussion*, Tito added conguero Carlos "Patato" Valdés to his core rhythm section and recorded the album with drums

The first cover for the 1955 Puente In Percussion album.

only (with the sole addition of the band's bassist, Machito alumnus Bobby Rodríguez). Tito explains how he put it together and how communication is the most important function of the drummer:

"I had the idea that I wanted to do a percussion album, just percussion. George Goldner couldn't see it. He said, 'How can you go in the studio and just play drums?' It took me a long

The second cover for the 1955 Puente In Percussion album.

The third cover for the 1955 Puente In Percussion album. Upper left: Mongo Santamaria. To the right: Tito. Lower left: Patato Valdés. Lower right: Willie Bobo.

time to convince him. I was always telling him that percussion sends a message. A percussion man is *saying* something. I explained to him about Africa, the mother country, where they used to send messages with their drums—you know, 'I got married,' 'Happy Birthday,' 'I went bankrupt, can you lend me five dollars?'—whatever. He got a big kick about my sense of humor about drumming.

"I said, 'George, look, we have the guys. They're all my friends. If we can all get together in the studio we can send a message on the bongos, on the congas, on the timbales and all that. Get them all in a circle, we can do it.' He still didn't want to do it. He said, 'What do you mean, no horns?' I said, 'Yeah, no horns, no trumpets, no saxes, no piano, no nothing, just drums.' I blew his mind with that. Finally, he wanted to make me happy. He said, 'I'm gonna give you the studio after midnight.' I said, 'That's okay, after midnight.'

"That album, we all sat around and stared at each other. Mongo brought in a bottle of Havana rum. We put it right there in the center and we had a little rum and planned the breaks and the endings to use after we finished our conversation with our drums. Everybody played great and that album turned out to be a classic—*Puente In Percussion.*"[12]

Released in 1955, Tito's first 12-inch 33 rpm album is a percussionist's dream, filled with timbale, bongo and conga solos, accents flying, beats displaced, as explosive and polyrhythmic as the fireworks on the Fourth of July, and as relentlessly energetic as the red jackhammer on the cover. "I had my chops built up at the time," says Tito.

Cuban Carnival and Top Percussion

In 1956, after recording eleven 10-inch albums with Tico, Tito signed with RCA. He never felt satisfied with his new label and had to pressure the executives to look after his interests. "They put me on the back burner. I finally had to go up to their offices and raise hell. After that they called me 'Little Caesar' at RCA."[13] Nevertheless, Tito made some of his most important records for the label, beginning with *Cuban Carnival*. For this album he added Cuban conguero Cándido Camero to the rhythm section. Cándido began his career as a guitar and bass player and later concentrated on bongos and congas. He came to New York and played with Duke Ellington and Dizzy Gillespie.

Original cover of the 1956 Cuban Carnival album.

Released in 1956, *Cuban Carnival* is a tour de force that goes straight to the roots of Afro-Cuban music, incorporating raw, infectious Cuban rhythms and jazz harmonies. It includes the classic up-tempo "Para Los Rumberos (For Dancers)," which also became a hit for Santana sixteen years later, and "Elegua Changó," a tune named for the Cuban Santeria deity, Changó, the god of thunder.

Top Percussion, released in 1957 as the follow-up to *Puente In Percussion*, features authentic Cuban rumba—religious-based percussion with chorus and vocal improvisation, no horns or melodic instruments of any kind—and includes Tito's classic timbale solo on "Ti Mon Bo." They came up with the name "Ti Mon Bo" by combining the first syllables of the names of the principal players, Tito, Mongo and Bobo. "Night Ritual," the track cut with a full band of horns and rhythm, features jazz drummer Jimmy Cobb on traps and trumpeter Doc Severinsen, later to be Johnny Carson's bandleader on *The Tonight Show*.

Original cover of the 1957 Top Percussion album.

Dance Mania

Tito became red hot in the late '50s, and *Dance Mania* was the album that lit the fire. Released in 1958, *Dance Mania* has been reissued twice, selling 500,000 copies by 1994. In January 2000, *The New York Times* listed the most significant albums of the 20th century, those representing turning points and pinnacles in popular music. *Dance Mania* was in the top 25. If *Puente In Percussion*

Cover of the reissue of the 1958 Dance Mania album.

was a drummer's dream, *Dance Mania* was a dancer's dream. The infectious rhythms coupled with Tito's slick, hard-hitting horn charts made every cut memorable. "There was no question about what Tito had done to the music," recalls Max Salazar. "He took it light-years ahead. When *Dance Mania* came out, that's all you heard for three years."

Tito knew how to make people dance. He understood horns and jazz harmonies and piano guajeos, but he also understood percussion. "Puente listens to the big band as a rhythm player, and he interprets the band as a drum," says conguero/trumpeter Jerry Gonzalez. Hilton Ruiz adds, "Tito's horn lines are percussive, based on the drum beats. You just add a melody and the whole band becomes a drum."[14] (The same thing was said in the '60s and '70s about one-time drummer James Brown's tight, danceable arrangements.) After *Dance Mania*, the votes came in and the contest was over. Tito had won. He was now officially the "King of Latin Music."

New Blood and Jazz

By this time Mongo Santamaria and Willie Bobo had left the band to play with Latin jazz vibist Cal Tjader. Bongocero Ray Rodríguez replaced Bobo in the percussion section and two José Curbelo alumni also arrived. Brooklyn-born Ray Barretto took Mongo's place on congas and Santos Colón began a fourteen-year stint as lead vocalist.

Tito's jazz side continued to flourish. He released *Puente Goes Jazz* in 1956, and although some accused him of trying to cross over, Tito had helped build the bridge in the first place. "Cross over?" he says. "I'm on my way back." The record sold 28,000 copies in two weeks. In 1958 he collaborated with Woody Herman for *Herman's Heat and Puente's Beat*.

One of Tito's many creative concepts was a little too creative for the less-than-adventurous "suits" at RCA. For the 1960 *Revolving Bandstand* album, Tito's band and trombonist Buddy Morrow's band faced off in the same studio at the same time. Morrow's group would play the first two eight-bar sections of "Autumn Leaves," for instance, in jazz style, and Tito's band would seamlessly enter and play the bridge in Latin style, and so on back and forth. How they managed to do it and keep the time is a mystery, but they did, and it works. RCA finally released the album in the U.S. in 1993!

End of an Era: Rock 'n' Roll and Boogaloo

One night at the Palladium in April 1961, as Pete Hamill reported in the *New York Daily News*, "The lights went on and there were cops everywhere, and skag, grass, works and shivs were falling to the floor all over the room…The cops arrested Rolande La Serie, the Cuban singer, and 14 other people on a variety of charges…a month later the liquor license was gone and the Palladium era was over."[15]

The Palladium was gone, but by this time Tito had his own audience all over the country and the beginnings of worldwide recognition. He continued to record, notably with the famous Cuban vocalist La Lupe, and began a fruitful relationship with Celia Cruz, one of many artists who

Tito at the timbales circa 1965.

fled Castro's regime in Cuba in the early '60s. Celia had sung at the Tropicana Casino in Havana throughout the '50s and had toured South and Central America and Mexico. She recorded six albums with Tito, and her vivacious vocal style has won her the title "The Queen of Latin Music."

Tito continued to work hotels and other large concert venues, but lesser-known Latin artists didn't fare so well as a new musical trend, begun in the early 1950s, captured the allegiance of America's youth. Elvis Presley, Chuck Berry, Fats Domino, Little Richard and the heavy backbeat of drummer Earl Palmer had the kids dancing to a new groove: rock 'n' roll. Rock 'n' roll originally incorporated conga rhythms on the drumset and pseudo-clave bass lines, but by the '60s it had developed an eminently danceable rhythm & blues beat of its own. The dominance of rock 'n' roll made it difficult for many Latin musicians to find work.

Cover of the the reissue of the 1960 Revolving Bandstand album.

Latino teenagers in El Barrio couldn't help but be influenced by the black rhythm & blues of nearby Harlem, so one solution for Latin bandleaders was Boogaloo (or bugalú), an attempt to combine Latin music with R&B. Among boogaloo's biggest hits were Ray Barretto's 1962 million seller, "El Watusi" (answered in the rock 'n' roll world by the Orlons' "Wah Wah Watusi"), Joe Cuba's million-selling "Bang Bang" and Mongo Santamaria's "Watermelon Man." Tito says the fad meant nothing to him. "It hurt the established bandleaders. They didn't want to record boogaloo but they had to in order to keep with the times." By 1969 boogaloo was dead.

Charangas and Típicas

Other new artists appeared on the scene, many of them former members of Tito's band like Charlie Palmieri. Charlie's band, Duboney, had a charanga format, a more traditional Cuban instrumentation that replaced the trumpets and saxes with strings and flute. After the Cuban revolution of 1959, Cuban musicians could no longer tour in the States, and Cuban-Americans longed to hear this traditional Cuban style. Eddie Palmieri, Charlie's younger brother, founded his first charanga group, La Perfecta, in 1961. Johnny Pacheco, who had played percussion with Tito's band and then flute with Charlie Palmieri, formed his own band. Another former Puente percussionist,

Tito performing with Cachao on bass and Miguelito Valdés on vocals in 1970 at the Tijuana Cat, NYC.

Ray Barretto, also became a leader.

The same longing for Cuban music also gave rise to the New York típicas, bands that replaced the charanga's strings and flutes with two trumpets and sometimes a trombone. Eddie Palmieri, Willie Colón and Típica '73 were prime examples of the típica style.

The típicas continued to combine jazz and advanced improvisational techniques with traditional rhythmic structures, just as Tito had done in the '50s.

Tito kept going his own way into the '70s largely unaffected by these new developments. He was, after all, the King, and people still flocked to his concerts. They wanted to hear Tito Puente, not the passing fads of the day. He took his band to Japan for the first time, and he had his own TV show, *El Mundo de Tito Puente*. He dodged around the pachanga, another fad, that quickly died because the dance was too exhausting for popular consumption. When the legendary Fania All-Stars recorded live at the Red Garter in the Village in 1972, Tito was there along with all the newer stars of the day, Eddie Palmieri, Johnny Pacheco and Larry Harlow.

What Is This Thing Called Salsa?

Suddenly in the '70s, there arrived a brand new phenomenon: SALSA!!! People tell many tales of how the name salsa, "sauce" in Spanish, got started. Some say salsa began with the

Cuban band Septeto Nacional and a song called "Echale Salsita," but others say *Latin New York* magazine publisher Izzy Sanabria began using it while emceeing a Fania All-Stars concert. Still others point to the cover of Cal Tjader's successful album, *Soul Sauce*, which features a bottle of red Louisiana hot sauce.

Established Latin musicians considered the name one more marketing ploy and resented the fact that their music was now being called something else. "There's no salsa music," Tito says.

Tito in a 1978 promotional shot for Latin Percussion.

"They just put that word to the music that we were doing all the time. The mambo, the cha cha, they called it 'salsa.' You *eat* salsa. You don't listen to it, you don't dance to it. But the word became so popular that people ask me, 'Tito, could you play me a salsa?' So I say, 'Do you have a headache? I'll give you an Alka-Seltzer.' They gave that name to the music to give it heat, make it exciting. It's easy for everybody to say. In my concerts I always tell everybody, 'Now, we're gonna play for you—SALSA!' The audience goes, 'OHHH!' It's the same mambo I've been playing for forty years."[16] Evelio M. Echemendeia put Tito's sentiments in a verse to a poem:

"Salsa Already Existed"
...And you have Tito Puente,
with his kinky mane,
beating fire out of the skin
of the very Cuban timbal,
saying, "That isn't new.
That thing called salsa doesn't go.
It's Afro-Cuban music
of many years ago."[17]

It may be the same mambo that Tito had been playing for forty years, but the name "salsa" did increase worldwide awareness of

Latin music. Tito didn't object when record sales rocketed to an all-time high or when the royalty checks for a cha-cha he had recorded fifteen years earlier suddenly started to amount to six figures.

Santana

In 1971 a San Francisco band, Santana, recorded a version of Tito's "Oye Como Va" which became a worldwide hit and gave Tito's career another boost. Santana's leader, guitarist Carlos Santana, a Mexican-born American son of a mariachi violinist, was influenced by the blues and R&B around him in San Francisco, but also connected with his Latin roots. Santana became popular after appearing at the original Woodstock Festival of 1969, and their version of Willie Bobo's "Evil Ways" on their first album, *Santana*, became a big hit. Santana's second album, *Abraxas*, included a version of Tito's infectious 1956 cha cha, "Oye Como Va" ("Listen To How It Goes"), which became an even bigger hit. The single went to number 13 on the *Billboard* pop charts and the song became a classic anthem for rock and salsa bands alike, a must for every Top 40 band in the country.

"'Oye Como Va' is a tune known all over the world," says Tito. "Everybody's played that tune. And," he adds jokingly, "if you don't play that tune in your repertoire, that means that you're not into nothin', see!?" Most people didn't realize that Tito wrote the song, and he gets asked, "Do you know that Santana tune, 'Oye Como Va'?" Santana also recorded Tito's 1956 original "Pa' Los Rumberos" on their third album, *Santana III*, in 1972. Carlos Santana's worldwide success greatly benefitted Tito, and in 1977 the Mambo King and the rock star performed together at New York's Roseland Ballroom.

LP Jazz Ensemble

In the disco '70s, computer-generated sounds and singers made most of the music heard on the radio; drum machines laid down repetitive dance grooves, the bass drum pounding relentlessly on all four quarter notes. Live musicians found it harder and harder to make ends meet. Tito suffered along with the others, but one new project, Martin Cohen's Latin Percussion

Tito at the right in 1978 with the Latin Percussion Jazz Ensemble performing in Japan with Dizzy Gillespie, a guest, top.

Jazz Ensemble, proved that he didn't have to worry: he was more popular internationally than he had ever imagined. Cohen had founded the musical instrument company Latin Percussion (LP), makers of congas, timbales, cowbells and other percussion instruments. LP modeled their first timbales on a set Tito brought back from Cuba: he had endorsed their timbales and been the focal point of their advertising campaign, "Trust the Leader." Cohen put together the LP Jazz Ensemble to play concerts, conduct seminars and promote LP products. Johnny Rodríguez, Tito's bongo player at the time, convinced Tito to join the project, which also included Carlos "Patato" Valdés on congas, Eddie Martinez on piano, and Sal Cuevas on electric bass. The group toured extensively in Europe and Japan in the '70s, and on these tours Tito realized Latin music had become a widespread phenomenon. His name was known around the world.

First Grammy

After his *The Legend* album got nominated for a Grammy in 1978, Tito won his first Grammy in 1979 for the album, *Homenage a Beny Moré* ("Homage to Beny Moré"). Moré, the

Cover of Tito's 1983 Grammy-winning album On Broadway.

famous Cuban singer, guitarist and composer, performed in Havana in the '40s, went to Mexico in 1945, joined the Perez Prado Orchestra, and then returned to Cuba to form his own band. Considered one of the greatest Latin singers of all time, he died in 1963 at the age of 43.

Puente's tribute album included several classic compositions by Moré, sung by a talented group including Celia Cruz, Santos Colón, Cheo Feliciano and Ismael Quintana.

To celebrate Tito's Grammy, *Latin New York* magazine roasted him at a dinner. One unexpected outcome of the dinner became one of Tito's favorite projects, his scholarship fund. According to Joe Conzo, Tito's long-time friend and archivist, "We received all of these checks given by the patrons of the roast, and we didn't know what to do with them, so we decided to set up a scholarship fund in Tito's name to help support the education of musically gifted youth."[18] Annual fund-raising concerts with Tito and top Latin artists support the Tito Puente Scholarship Fund. Originally associated with the Juilliard School of Music, the scholarship fund now calls Spanish Harlem's Boys Harbor Music Conservatory home. Since Tito took every chance to study music as a boy and has always demanded first-class musicianship from his band members, it's not surprising that he would encourage the youth of the Latin community to study their musical traditions.

Cover of the 1984 El Rey album.

As he started this scholarship for kids, Tito began receiving awards himself as the elder statesman of Latin music. In 1979 he played for President Carter to benefit the Congressional Hispanic Caucus, and what better song to play, since Carter was a peanut farmer, than Moises Simons' classic, "El Manisero" ("The Peanut Vendor")? Tito later played for Presidents Reagan, Bush and Clinton. He's been given the keys to the cities of New York, Miami and Los Angeles. He's fond of these awards, which his wife Margie

Cover of the 1985 Grammy-winning Mambo Diablo album.

encourages him to put in the garage of their New York suburban home, "along with all that other stuff," but he jokingly adds, "I'm still waiting for someone to give me the keys to a bank!"[19]

1980s: The Tito Puente Latin Jazz Ensemble and Concord Records

As Tito became more involved in the LP Jazz Ensemble, it was renamed the Tito Puente Latin Jazz Ensemble, and later Tito Puente and His Latin Ensemble. The expanded instrumentation of the Latin Ensemble included Jimmy Frisaura on trumpet and trombone, Ray Gonzalez on trumpet, Mario Rivera on saxophones and flute, Alfredo De La Fé on violin, Jerry Gonzalez on congas and flugelhorn, Edgardo Miranda on guitar and cuatro,

Tito playing with the Tito Puente Latin Jazz Ensemble. Jerry Gonzalez is on congas to the right.

Jorge Dalto on piano, Bobby Rodríguez on Fender bass and Johnny Rodríguez on bongos. Tito was featured on timbales and vibes. This became a perfect vehicle for "the old man," as he was now known, to channel his seemingly endless writing and performing energies.

Concord Records' Picante label was beginning to make a name for itself in the Latin jazz field and at Cal Tjader's suggestion they signed Tito and this expanded band, a wise and profitable decision. Tito's first Picante release, *On Broadway*, won another Grammy in 1983. The next Concord Picante album, *El Rey*, kept the expanded line-up with the substitution of Francisco Aguabella on congas and José Madera Jr. on congas and timbales. A successful and innovative adventure in the world of Latin jazz, this record included Latin versions of the John Coltrane classics "Giant Steps" and "Equinox," harking back to the days when Tito played opposite "Trane" at Birdland. Tito received his third Grammy for his third Picante album, *Mambo Diablo*, released in 1985, which continued to combine the best of Latin and jazz. For this, Tito brought out his "venetian blinds" and played a sensitive and smokey version of Billy Strayhorn's "Lush Life."

The Mambo Kings and the 100th Album

Comfortable in the role of entertainer, Tito appeared in several late '80s movies more legitimate than the *Cuban Pete* films of his screen debut: John Candy's *Armed and Dangerous* and Woody Allen's *Radio Days*. He also appeared on several TV shows, including a memorable episode of *The Bill Cosby Show* with Patato, Art Blakey and Percy Heath, when Cosby goaded everyone into a jam session. Tito also added a fourth Grammy to his collection with the 1989 album, *Goza mi timbal*, and in 1990 he was honored with a star on Hollywood's Walk of Fame.

Yet it was the movie *The Mambo Kings* in 1991 that pushed

Tito's fame to a new level. As Joe Conzo explains, "That two minutes he was on the screen in *The Mambo Kings* put him in another ball park."[20] The film, based on the Pulitzer Prize-winning novel *The Mambo Kings Play Songs of Love,* by Oscar Hijuelos, tells the story of two musicians, Cesar Castillo and his brother Nestor, who came to New York from Cuba in the '50s to "make it" in the Latin music scene. They head first for the Palladium, and who should they find on the bandstand playing a swinging mambo?—the "King of the Mambo," of course. Playing himself in the film, Tito lets the pushy Cesar, played by Armand Assante, finagle his way onto the bandstand, take his sticks and play a timbale solo—an incident that could never have happened in real life, any more than a fan could have asked Elvis, "Hey, man, can I sing one?" But *The Mambo Kings* successfully re-created the atmosphere of the Palladium and the New York Latin scene in the '50s, and the movie became tremendously popular.* The resulting publicity brought Tito recognition on an even wider scale.

Cover of the 1991 *The Mambo King* album, Tito's 100th LP.

Pegged to the film, Tito released the album *The Mambo King,* his 100th album (not including reissues or re-packaged "best of 's"), a unique accomplishment. "A lot of people say they've done 100 albums," says TP, "but we checked and didn't find anybody else with that many. I got 100 and you can look it up."[21] The album's version of Tito's classic, "Ran Kan Kan," made *Billboard's* Top Ten Club Playlist in 1991, forty-two years after its original release in 1949!

Cover of the program for the 1996 Tito Puente Scholarship Fund concert. Tito calls this the "Before and After" photo.

The Golden Latin Jazz All-Stars

Other performing opportunities continued to pour in up to and past the millennium: dates with Sheila E., Arturo Sandoval, Poncho Sanchez, Tower of Power, Plácido Domingo and Gloria Estefan. Tito had come a long way from his Spanish Harlem beginnings and he shows no signs of letting up. He

*Joe Conzo also appears in the Palladium scene as a thug who murders one of the patrons, clearing the dance floor and sending the crowd to the exits.

continues to front his traditional Latin Orchestra as well as his Latin Jazz Ensemble, now known as the Golden Latin Jazz All-Stars, in which he plays with the best of a new generation of Latin musicians: saxophonist Paquito d'Rivera, a former member of Cuba's Irakére; Puerto Rican master conguero Giovanni Hidalgo; flutist Dave Valentin; trumpeter Claudio Roditi; conservatory-trained piano wiz Hilton Ruiz; and versatile drumset player Ignacio Berroa.

"I've got two bands," Tito explains tongue-in-cheek, "which means I've got two headaches. One is the Latin-Jazz Ensemble, eight or so pieces, and the other is the Tito Puente Orchestra, fourteen or so pieces. Some audiences want more jazz, some more Latin. I'm ready for whatever."

Conclusion

*"All right, Tito Puente,
show the world that you
are really the king of the timbal.
All right, Tito Puente, let go now
the blast that
I pay you for. Now Tito!
Beat your timbal...
Eee, beat it, beat it, beat it,
beat it, beat it.
Tito, I leave it to you."*
—*Celia Cruz (singing "Celia y Tito" from* The Mambo King *album)*

The timbales are a Cuban instrument, but according to a leading Cuban musicologist, Dr. Olavo Alén Rodríguez, "The greatest timbale player in the world is not a Cuban. He's Puerto Rican. Cuba has many, many very good timbale players, but in the international arena none of them could compete with Tito Puente."

Tito has been described as a temperamental artist, a disciplinarian who strives for perfection and quality in all his recordings to the point of alienating his men. Yet once the recording, rehearsal or gig is over, TP relaxes and becomes a regular guy. "The man bears malice toward no one," says one colleague.[22] Hilton Ruiz adds, "A life force emanates from music that makes us feel good. As musicians I feel that we are spiritual healers, and Tito definitely has that power."[23]

Tito Puente has had more than fifty years of experience in the music business. He has released 116 albums to date. He performs in thirty jazz festivals each year and has played an estimated 10,000 engagements over the course of his career. Whenever and wherever people hear his music, they can't resist moving to the beat—they get up and dance. Crowds continue to be electrified by the charming gentleman with the shining eyes, infectious smile and thick shock of pure white hair.

Tito and his wife, Margie, in 1993.

For all his fame, Tito Puente remained a modest man totally dedicated to music. *Latin Times* magazine held a dinner in his honor in 1977 and after several people had praised him, Tito unfolded a piece of paper he had in his pocket and began to speak:

"I have tried my best to expose our music and to bring enjoyment and pride to our Latin people, to the young people. The young bandleaders, some of these guys do not know the chord changes, they miss the flatted fifths, and I know they do. At times I have jumped on them. I don't anymore. But whenever they asked me, I corrected them. When they played well I never said a thing. When they played great I didn't even say 'Good evening.' But when they goofed, I jumped on their backs.

"So the best thing is either you stay and learn and go to school, or take a walk. Put our music where it is supposed to be. To the young people struggling to make something of themselves, I urge you to study your craft and work as hard as you can. Nothing, believe me, comes easy. I ought to know. I studied. I am a graduate of the conservatory of Juilliard. I have my books, I have my diploma. As a musician my work has denied me. I've spent lonesome holidays away from my family and lost many hours of sunshine. But I do not regret it because an artist must do what he feels…it was something I felt I had to do. If my music has brought joy to one person, then I have been successful."[24]

Tito with Jimmy Frisaura on trumpet, Mongo Santamaria on congas & Gilberto Monroig on bongo bell. A New York theater, 1953.

Nicky Marrero and Tito battle it out on timbales in California in the late '80s.

A Brief History.

of Afro-Cuban Music

"Cuban music is voices and drums, the rest is a luxury."
—Orlando Marin, bandleader.

W HEN THE SPANISH CAME TO THE NEW WORLD IN THE
1500S, THEY COLONIZED A LARGE ISLAND NAMED
CUBANICAN OR "CENTER PLACE." ITS LONG, NARROW
LAND MASS LAY BETWEEN FLORIDA TO THE NORTH, SANTO
DOMINGO AND PUERTO RICO TO THE EAST, JAMAICA TO
THE SOUTH, AND MEXICO TO THE WEST. THROUGH FIVE CENTURIES,
CUBA HAS REMAINED THE CROSSROADS OF THE CARIBBEAN, SENDING
ITS FINE SUGARS AND TOBACCOS TO THE WORLD and accepting to its
shores waves of settlers from many races and nations.

Any melting pot of cultures becomes a melting pot of music,
and Cuba is no exception. People as different as aristocrats from
France and slaves from the Congo; deities as distinct as Mary the
Virgin Mother and Chango the God of Thunder; cities as unlike
as Havana and Hollywood; musical instruments as diverse as
codfish crates and violins; dances as different as the minuet and
the mambo—all have contributed their colors and flavors to the
fascinating stew that is Cuban music.

It's hard to pin down the beginnings of a music composed
from so many blended elements, but the heart of Cuban music is a
combination of Africa and Europe: Africa contributed its rhythmic
percussion and vocal chants, and Europe its melodic instruments,
songs and dances.

Through much of its history, Cuba has been a poor country.
Centuries of making do have taught the proud and resourceful
Cuban people that you don't need much to have a good time
making music. If you didn't have a drum, a good-sounding wooden
box would do, or a cowbell, even a hoe blade; to the beats of these
instruments, men or women could dance and sing stories of their
sufferings and joys. When that music of the rural peasants and
African slaves mingled with the music of the urban upper class
a century and more ago, modern Cuban music, now known and
loved around the world as salsa, was born.

I-African Roots
Black Gods Are Dancing Gods.[1]

Soon after Columbus discovered the Americas, colonists from Spain, France and England began bringing Africans from Nigeria, Dahomey, the Congo and many other nations to the New World as slaves. If they survived the gruelling trip in the holds of sailing ships, they were soon bought by planters and put to work as laborers in the fields, growing the sugar and tobacco which would enrich their new owners but not themselves. African slaves, working beside enslaved native Indians, helped make Cuba the world's largest sugar producer; its tobacco is still used to make the finest cigars in the world.

The climate was sweltering hot, the work backbreaking, and the living conditions minimal, but the African slaves survived and even managed to hold on to their culture.

Santería: Religious Percussion Music

Drums played a major role in African culture. The Spanish feared the African drums, didn't understand their messages, and thought that the drums could be used to incite the slaves to rebellion. So they banned the drums and tried to convert the Africans to Christianity and assimilate them into Western culture—this was considered an essential part of colonization.

The Africans resisted. They had their own religion, **Santería**, and their own deities to which they continued to pray, though disguised as Christian saints. The religion of the Yoruba people of Africa, known in Cuba as Lucumis, Santería has a variety of rituals and festivities all based on certain rhythms and drums, combined with other wood and metal sounds.

To help each other survive slavery and to preserve their cultural roots, the Yorubas formed societies called **cabildos**, each cabildo led by a god-father or a god-mother whose private home was their meeting place, the temple home. Yorubans called their deities *Orishas*. In festivities known as "toques para los santos" (beats for the saints), they used and still use drums to call for the aid or assistance of the Orishas—Elegguá, for example, the guardian of the crossroads, the gatekeeper of the intersection between the

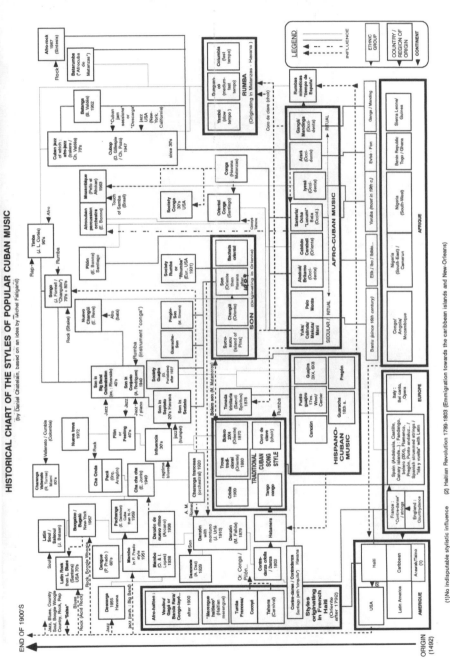

HISTORICAL CHART OF THE STYLES OF POPULAR CUBAN MUSIC
(by Daniel Chatelain, based on an idea by Michel Faligand)

First version publication : PERCUSSIONS review n° 44 (Paris, 1996), updated version 01 2000 © Daniel Chatelain

(1) No indisputable stylistic influence   (2) Haitian Revolution 1789-1803 (Emmigration towards the caribbean islands and New-Orleans)

material and spiritual planes.

The double-headed **batá drums** used to call the gods come three in a set. They are considered sacred and are designed to reproduce the tonal changes and speech patterns of the Yoruba language. The gods live in the drums; drummers summon them to come out and take possession of the people participating in the ritual.

The largest batá drum is called the iyá or mother drum, the middle drum is the **itótele**, and the smallest is called the **okónkolo.** The batá singer is known as the **gallo** or rooster. Santería ritual allows improvisation on some drums, but many drums are considered baptized when first made, and the players can only play certain **toques**, or rhythms, on them. "There are certain rhythms you wouldn't apply outside the ceremony," explains percussionist Milton Cardona. "Some rhythms you can jam on, but there are certain deities that you wouldn't want to mess with."[2]

The secret societies known as **abakuá** (sometimes spelled "abakwa") have their own sacred rhythms and rituals as well. Among other drums, they use the **ekué drum,** which is rubbed with a thin rod to produce a low sound. The magic voice which comes out of the drum is then interpreted by a shaman or priest.

Slaves from the Congo brought their drums—**tumbadoras***—played in conjunction with **hoe blades** (actual blades of farming hoes) and **cowbells.** Wood sounds such as sticks on the sides of congas and **claves** are also used, as well as various **shakers** and **bass drums.**

Rumba

"The rumba...people confuse that word with rhumba with an 'h,' a slower commercial style that Xavier Cugat used to play—tunes like 'Begin the Beguine.'" —TP

Rumba, or Lay Rumba as it's sometimes called, is the non-religious side of the percussion music brought to Cuba by the African slaves. After slavery was abolished in 1886, many poor Cubans moved into larger cities looking for work, settling in the cheaper districts. When they wanted to party or celebrate, they played rumba, dancing, drumming and singing on the street corners. In the rumbas they could discuss neighborhood affairs, including gossip about the latest infidelities.

At first they played on boxes and bureau drawers turned upside down, then they began using the crates used to ship salted

* Americans later called them congas when they saw them played in a dance called the Conga.

codfish. To improve the sound they took the rough crates apart, sanded them and put them back together, eliminating the cracks. Eventually they replaced the crates with congas or tumbadoras, but some groups still use crates today.

The basic form of rumba has remained constant over the years. A vocalist sings and plays claves while the drummers play and sing as a chorus in response to the lead. Another musician plays the **cáscara** rhythm with two sticks, either on the side of a conga, or on a small wooden box, or on a mounted, hollowed-out piece of wood called a **catá**. Modern-day timbale players have borrowed the cáscara rhythm directly from the rumba groups. Rumba players move freely from drum to drum, and each drummer is usually proficient in all the various parts. The singers can also sit down and play the drums.

Rumba has three main styles: **Guaguanco, Columbia** and **Yambú**. The Yambú style, nearly extinct today, was originally played on candle and codfish packing crates. To add a higher-pitched sound, players struck a bottle with a coin. Columbia is based on a fast-paced, 6/8 rhythm in which a single male dancer challenges the lead **quinto** drummer to a rhythmic battle. The quinto is the smaller, higher-pitched lead drum of the group. Two male dancers can also challenge each other in Columbia. Guaguanco, which has its origin in a Congolese fertility dance, features a dance between a man and a woman in which the woman tries to avoid the sexual advances of the man—an acting out of the universal game of courtship that we all know so well. The **Conga** is another form of African dance, performed in street carnivals by groups of dancers and percussionists known as **comparsas**.

Throughout the developments and transformations from the beginning up to the present day, the rhythm of Afro-Cuban music has always been firmly based on the rumba tradition. If you combine the rhythmic elements of rumba with Son (see below), you have much of what is considered Cuban popular music or salsa today.

II-Spanish and European Roots

If the Africans supplied the drums of Cuban music, what did the Europeans supply? Spanish Catholics brought church music and trained singers and musicians to sing and play it on church pianos and organs. The Spanish government brought military music played by the army bands on snare drums and brass instruments. The Spanish and French also brought the music of the European courts, the violin music of the minuets and quadrilles heard coming from the houses of the upper classes. The poor Spanish peasants, or campesinos, brought their canciones, songs with a verse-chorus structure played on the guitar and the tres, a smaller, three-stringed guitar. All of these musical forms eventually became Africanized with the addition of African percussion.

Son

There is no Son without the claves.[3]

Perhaps the most influential of all the early forms of Cuban music is the **Son**, a combination of the African music of the slaves and the Spanish music of the campesinos, African percussion added to Spanish songs played on stringed instruments.

The early Sons, called **Changuí**, developed among the people in Oriente Province, in the eastern end of Cuba, during the second half of the 19th century. Musicians played these Spanish canciones or songs using the **tres,** a three-stringed guitar; the **marimbula,** a box similar to an African thumb piano, only larger and used for the bass notes; and **claves, guiro, maracas** and **bongos**. In some cases the **botija**, a clay jug, was also used for bass sounds. Because Son groups used six instruments—tres, marimbula, guiro, maracas, claves and bongos—they were known as **Sextetos**. All the musicians sang as well. As the Son developed out of Changuí, the string bass replaced the marimbula and the guitar replaced the tres.

The Son originally had an unsavory reputation. People used these musical gatherings to air out pet peeves and frustrations. Often the lyrics would discuss a daughter's virginity, a wife's infidelity or someone's ugliness, and sometimes fights broke out. The government considered the music immoral, but as the form developed, the lyrics were cleaned up for popular consumption.

By the 1920s the Son of Eastern Cuba was thriving in Havana, one of the most popular groups being the **Sexteto Habanero**, whose bassist, **Ignacio Piñero** (1886-1969), became an important figure in Cuban music. By 1927 Piñero was leading his own group, the **Septeto Nacional**—a Septeto because he added a trumpet as a seventh instrument to the format. The trumpet brought the sounds of the Spanish bull ring to Son and also the first sounds of the American jazz being played in New Orleans and other U.S. cities.

By the 1930s, trumpet-led septets and large jazz-type big bands were playing Son in the big Havana hotels that catered to North and South Americans seeking a vacation in the sun-filled tropics. **Benny Moré's Band** performed as part of lavish stage shows in the Hotel Nacionale and the Tropicana, providing employment for Cuban musicians and a place to test new styles of Cuban music. Moré's impassioned vocals made him one of the most influential Cuban soneros of all time. Many artists, including Tito Puente, have dedicated tribute albums to him.

The verse-chorus form of the Son (ABAB) was expanded when an extended chorus or **montuno** section was added. The A and B sections of the song, based on the European closed form, had a fixed number of measures. The montuno was an open vamp section based on a rural tradition (montuno means "from the mountains"), in which the lead singer and chorus continued in call-and-response fashion until the lead singer ran out of things to say. The addition of the montuno section represented a major change in the Son form and led to several important developments, as we shall see.

Danzón

Now let's examine the history of Danzón, the second major style that merged with the Son to create much of what we know today as salsa. The Danzón evolved in stages: **Contradanse-Danza-Danzón-Cha cha chá.**

The **Contradanse** (or country dance) has French roots. After the 1781 slave rebellion on the French colonial island of Haiti, Cuba's closest eastern neighbor, Haitian slaves and others who wanted to leave the island and start over again migrated to the eastern tip of Cuba, Oriente Province. In 1812, when President Thomas Jefferson convinced Napoleon to sell the Louisiana Purchase to the United States, many French people from New Orleans also decided to move their households to Cuba.

The new arrivals from Haiti and New Orleans brought the Contradanse to Cuba. Originally a European high-society dance, the Contradanse was an instrumental dance music, played with piano, violins, and flutes, to which couples danced while holding each other in an embrace. This was not done in Africa and meant a major departure from the solo dances and the challenge dances of the rumba tradition. The original instrumentation of piano, violins and flutes was augmented with clarinets, trumpets, güiro and tympani, and the name Contradanse was changed to the Spanish spelling, **Contradanza**. The Contradanzas were usually played outdoors by groups called **Orquestas Típicas** or "typical orchestras." Later they were played indoors for more sedate events by groups called **Charangas**, or **Charanga Francesas** (French orchestras), who chose the quieter instrumentation of wooden flutes, violins, string bass, güiro and smaller tympani called **timbales Criollos**, or **Creole tympani**.

These Creole tympani, smaller and easier to carry around than the traditional European symphonic tympani, were the precursers of our modern-day timbales. The first timbales Criollos may have been made from iron or copper vessels in the shape of half a grapefruit used to hold the guarapo (juice) of the sugarcane.[4] Sticks were used to play on the heads and sides of the timbales Criollos, using a technique known as **baqueteo** in which the hands were also pressed on the heads so that the sticks could produce muffled sounds and different pitches. These smaller timbales were also called **pailas Cubanas** (Cuban pailas) or, simply, **pailas**. Many people in Cuba still use the name pailas when referring to the modern-day, single-headed, open-bottomed timbales.

The Contradanza, incorporating the so-called **habanera** or **cinquillo rhythm**, $|\frac{2}{4} \, \flat \, \flat$ 𝄽 𝄞 𝄽 $|$*, on the Creole tympani or pailas, eventually evolved into the **Danza**, which became popular with the upper classes. When the dancers wanted the dances to last longer, more sections were added to the Danza and it became the **Danzón**, or "large dance." **Miguel Failde** is credited with the composition of the first Danzón, "**Las Alturas de Simpson**," in 1879, which incorporated the cinquillo rhythm in the Creole tympani, violin and flute parts. Danzón took the form ABAC: A, the paseo or introduction in which the dancers promenaded around the dance floor, B the flute melody, and C the solo section for strings. Again, couples, for the most part, danced in an

* Drummer David Garibaldi described this rhythm to me as the King Kong beat, a popular funk ride cymbal and hihat pattern played in Oakland, California, in the '70s. It was derived from the song "King Kong," by the group Redbone, which was led by two Native-American brothers, Pat and Lolly Vega. The King Kong beat is the same as the five-note habanera rhythm, also called the cinquillo.

embrace following the European tradition.

At the end of the 19th century, the Danzón of high society merged with the Son from the streets and rural areas, giving birth to the 20th-century **mambo** and **cha cha chá**.* Here we see the value of the continual cross-fertilization between the various Cuban styles. Always the "center place" of the Caribbean, Cuba "Africanized" European music and "Europeanized" African music. The African percussion instruments were added to the European melodic instruments: the guitar, the violin, the trumpet and later the piano. The Son with its bongos, from the streets and rural areas, merged with the Danzón and its timbales, from high society and the city. Such roots create a rich texture of rhythm and music, the cultural heritage of a proud and resourceful people.

III-Afro-Cuban Music in the 20th Century~Tin Pan Alley and Hollywood

In 1930 **Don Azpiazú's Havana Casino Orchestra** recorded a version of Moises Simon's "**The Peanut Vendor**" for RCA. At first, the company thought it was too strange for American ears, but when finally released, "The Peanut Vendor" quickly became a national hit and helped spawn the so-called "rhumba craze." Americans used the word rhumba, spelled with an "h," indiscriminately to describe any music with a remotely Latin sound. By 1932 E.B. Marks music publishers had 600 Latin-American songs in their catalog. Even George Gershwin wrote a "Cuban Overture," and many others jumped on the band wagon to try to cash in on the new style.

"Cashing in": two words that epitomized the early efforts by Hollywood to introduce Americans to Latin music. The movie image of Latin music in the U.S. blended palm trees, exotic island romance, dark-skinned beauties and handsome Latin lovers—a fiction invented by Hollywood for popular consumption and bearing little resemblance to the professional, down-to-earth music scene in Cuba.

One who suited Hollywood's marketing plan for the new Latin sound and cashed in the most was the Spaniard **Xavier Cugat**.

* The Danzón tradition lives on today as the slower, softer, more romantic element in various Cuban styles, including Canción trovadoresca or troubador songs; Guajira (a la "Guantanamera"), songs featuring an idyllic view of the countryside, something like American country music; Bolero (slow, sweet, romantic songs); the more recent "Feeling" music (love ballads of the '50s and '60s), and the New Trova ('60s and '70s protest songs, using American pop harmonies).

A popular Latin bandleader in the '30s and '40s, Cugat catered to downtown, non-Latin audiences in New York's big hotels and supper clubs. He played at the opening of the Waldorf Astoria and stayed on as the resident orchestra there for many years, while also appearing in more films than any other American bandleader.

"Americans know nothing about Latin music," he explained in a 1950 interview. "They neither understand nor feel it, they have to be given music more for the eyes than the ears. Eighty percent visual, the rest aural."[5] Following this formula, Cugat always put a pretty woman in front of the band, Rita Hayworth being one of the most famous. Cugat made no bones about his approach with American audiences. "To succeed in America I gave the Americans a Latin music that had nothing authentic about it. Then I began to change the music and play more legitimately."[6]

The charming **Desi Arnaz**, son of a mayor of Santiago de Cuba and a conga player with Xavier Cugat when he first came to the States, also did much to shape the image of the Latin bandleader in the U.S. Richard Rodgers and Lorenz Hart saw Desi during an engagement at New York's La Conga club, and decided he'd be perfect for the Latin male lead in *Too Many Girls*, a 1939 Broadway show about the sex life of a South American football player in a U.S. college. In the show Desi played opposite his future wife, Lucille Ball. Together they went on to have one of the most successful television shows of all time, *I Love Lucy*.

Carmen Miranda (1909-1955) contributed a more bizarre image for Latin music in the United States. A radio and recording star in Rio de Janeiro, Carmen made her mark with her performance in the Broadway revue *On the Streets of Paris*, starring, of all people, Abbott and Costello! The first act finale featured Carmen singing and parading with a hat piled high with bananas, pineapples and various types of fruit. The fruit headdress became her trademark, and she went on to appear in many successful Hollywood productions.

That U.S. record companies considered Latin music a novelty is evident in the gimmicky titles of many songs, "A Little Rhumba Numba," "I Came I Saw I Conga'd" and Carmen Miranda's "Chiquita Banana," to name a few. Although Latin music's early image was neither respectful nor accurate, Hollywood and Broadway nevertheless exposed many people to the Latin style, and the popularity of the music increased.

Machito and Mario Bauzá

At the same time, serious Afro-Cuban musicians were interested in both preserving the authentic roots of the music and expanding and developing the genre. The godfather of legitimate Afro-Cuban music in the U.S. was **Machito**. Machito, born Frank Grillo, was one of the first authentic Cuban soneros, or singers, to be successful on the New York scene. He came to New York from Havana in 1937 and recorded with several bandleaders, including Xavier Cugat, before forming his own band, which opened at New York's **Club Conga** in 1940. Machito's sister, **Graciela**, was also a featured singer in the band, which was founded as a partnership between Machito and his musical director, **Mario Bauzá**.

Bauzá holds an important position in Afro-Cuban music, especially in the combination of Afro-Cuban music with American jazz, later known as **Cubop**. A brilliant and versatile musician, he began his career in the classical field playing bass clarinet with the **Havana Philharmonic**. After coming to the U.S. in 1930, he was introduced to the group **Cuarteto Machin**, a band getting ready to record and looking for a trumpet player. Bass clarinetist Bauzá wasn't fazed. He learned to play the trumpet in two weeks and played on the session! Next he got a job with **Noble**

Machito and His Afro-Cubans. This picture was taken during a 1948 Columbia Pictures movie short titled "Machito and his Rumba Band," which featured female singer Buddy Riley. Machito, center. First row from the left: Leslie Johnakins, baritone sax; José Pin Madera, tenor sax; Eugene Johnson, tenor sax; Fred Skeritt, alto sax; Armando Punzalen, tenor sax. Second row from the left: Jimmy Lawrence, Mario Bauzá, Bobby Woodland, trumpets; Fernando Arbelo, trombone/arranger; Humberto Gelabert, trombone. Third row from the left: Carlos Vidal, congas; José Mangual, bongos; Ubaldo Nieto, drumset; René Hernández, piano; Julio Andino, bass.

Sissle's Orchestra at the Park Central Hotel playing saxophone, going on to play with **Hi Clark and His Missourians,** and then with drummer Chick Webb's band as lead trumpeter in 1933. He became the band's director a year later. In 1939 Bauzá joined **Cab Calloway,** whose repertoire featured several Latin-influenced pieces, including "Minnie the Moocher." Thoroughly versed in all aspects of Cuban music, Bauzá was now becoming an expert in American jazz as well.

When he went into partnership with Machito to form **Machito and His Afro-Cubans,** Bauzá set out to bring together the best elements of Latin and jazz. "Our idea was to bring Latin music up to the standard of the American orchestras,"[7] he explained. He brought in **John Bartee** and other arrangers who had worked with Chick Webb and Cab Calloway, and their charts incorporated the most modern big band voicings for saxes and trumpets. The group perfected their sound for months in rehearsals before their first appearance. (Tito Puente no doubt saw them playing at the Park Plaza Ballroom opposite **Federico Pagani's Happy Boys.**) Machito and His Afro-Cubans set a high standard for Latin music for many years to come. They spent four years as the house band at La Conga on 53rd between 7th Ave. and Broadway, and played in many other venues for both the uptown Spanish audiences and the more ethnically diverse downtown audiences. Tito Puente played with Machito before being drafted into the Navy in 1942.

Machito's band kept the basic Cuban structure: first the "head" or main melody, then the montuno or vamp (in which a chorus sings repeated lines behind the lead singer or improvising instrumentalist). This section included new material for brass and saxes borrowed from the big band format and became known as the "mambo" section. After **Carlos Vidal** began playing congas in the band in 1943, that instrument became a permanent part of the rhythm section, reinforcing the bass and providing a solid foundation for the authentic Cuban sound.

The Mambo

The creation of the mambo is attributed to several different people. **Israel "Cachao" Lopez,** the bassist with **Arcaño y sus Maravillas,** a well-known Danzón orchestra, is the name most often mentioned first. Cachao added an open-ended improvisational vamp to the Danzón (a D section) and called it the **Nuevo Ritmo**, or "new rhythm" section. At first this new music was called **Danzón de nuevo ritmo** "Danzón with the new rhythm," then later it was called the mambo section. In the **mambo section,** violins played **guajeos** (repeated two bar figures), and the flutist, Arcaño, improvised above them in the higher register. Arcaño also added a conga drum to the rhythm section and, coupled with Cachao's strong **tumbaó**, or ostinato bass line, this gave the music an added rhythmic intensity. **Ulpanio Díaz**, Arcaño's timbale player, added a cowbell to his setup, which he played during this new section, also giving the music more drive and increased danceability. The fickle public rejected this new section at first, but in the 1940s Arcaño y sus Maravillas, with the influential piano player **Jésus Perez**, became Cuba's most popular band.

The second most influential musician in the development of the mambo was the blind guitarist **Arsenio Rodríguez** (1911-1970). A black Cuban of Congolese descent and a major Son bandleader during the '30s and '40s, Rodríguez was blinded in his youth when kicked in the head by a mule, but nevertheless he became a master tres player and composer. He was also an excellent percussionist, and is credited with introducing the conga drum and the hand-held **campana bell** to the Son conjuntos. The salsa rhythm section was now taking shape as the congas joined the bongos and new rhythms were introduced. Most importantly, Arsenio took the mambo rhythm, originally used in the Congolese-derived religious groups, and brought it into the dance halls.

Rodríguez came to New York in the '50s, originally to have an eye operation in an attempt to cure his blindness. The operation was unsuccessful but he stayed on in New York for the rest of his life, never returning to Cuba. His lyrics reflected the racial concerns of a proud man, and while he popularized the syncopated, mid-tempo **Son montuno,** his music was considered difficult and rather hard-sounding. Rodríguez never became very popular, but as is often the case, though the public didn't understand him, he strongly influenced his fellow musicians—Tito Puente, Eddie Palmieri and Larry Harlow, to name just a few.

Perez Prado, the third name that comes up when discussing the beginnings of the mambo, became wildly popular, though some consider his style of Cuban music commercialized and over-simplified. The Cuban pianist and organist took the newly developed mambo section and used it as the basis for his new style—in essence, he turned the mambo section into the entire song. Prado's big band jazz instrumentation, featuring saxes and trumpets, showed the influence of Duke Ellington, Count Basie and Chick Webb. Prado had little success in Cuba, as critics mercilessly opposed his new style, but in 1949 he left his home country and went to Mexico, where he became popular. He made many successful tours of the U.S. beginning in 1951, and had several hit recordings, including two that made it to number one on the *Billboard* Top Pop Singles charts: "Cherry Pink and Apple Blossom White" (1955) and "Patricia" (1958).

Invented by Israel "Cachao" Lopez and Arsenio Rodríguez, and popularized by Perez Prado, the mambo became the perfect vehicle for the New York Latin big band instrumentation of four trumpets, four saxes and four trombones. Machito led the way as the mambo became the dance craze that swept the country, but there were two other bandleaders besides Machito who made up the so-called "Big Three" of the mambo—Tito Rodríguez and Tito Puente. Now our brief history parallels Tito Puente's own biography (see biography section), as he began to ride and contribute to all the new waves of Afro-Cuban music.

Following the example of Machito and Mario Bauzá, Tito combined the big band format with Cuban percussion and created an infectious dance music that insured him an important place in the history of Afro-Cuban music. He brought the timbales out in front of the band and played them standing up in order to give his cues more easily, now the accepted method of playing the instrument. His fiery solos captivated audiences and established a new standard for technique and musicality, as his band and the other two members of the "Big Three" kept the people dancing throughout the heyday of the mambo.

Cha Cha Chá

While the fast-paced mambo was sweeping the country in the '40s and '50s, a new, slower-paced dance called the cha cha chá became nearly as popular. The cha cha chá evolved from the nuevo ritmo section of the Danzón, and got its name from the shuffling sound of the dancers' feet. Vocals were added to this slower-paced music, "infinitely easier to dance than mambo,"[8] and a straight quarter-note pulse on the cha cha bell replaced the traditional cinquillo rhythm of the Danzón. The first cha

cha chá, "**La Engañadora**," was written in 1951 by the Cuban violinist **Enrique Jorrín**, formerly a member of Arcaño y sus Maravillas, and was played by the Cuban charangas with strings, flute, bass, güiro, timbales and congas. **Orquesta Aragón** and flutist **José Fajardo** also popularized the cha cha chá in Cuba in the '50s.

Soon after the big bands in the Havana casinos featured this infectious dance, the cha cha chá migrated to the U.S. and became a staple in the repertoire of the "Big Three," and all Latin bandleaders. Perhaps the best-known Latin tune of all time is Tito Puente's classic cha cha chá "Oye Como Va," which Carlos Santana made internationally famous in the '70s.

The "Big Three" of Latin music. From the left: Tito Rodríguez, Machito and Tito Puente.

Cubop and Latin Jazz

As Latin rhythms and big band harmonies culminated in the flowering of the mambo and the cha cha chá at the Palladium, down the block from a smaller club called **Birdland**, a powerful new jazz movement was taking shape: bebop. The new small groups (quartets and quintets) were put together out of necessity when changing times made it harder economically to support the big bands. Jazz musicians were also fueled by a desire to experiment with more avant-garde harmonies and freer rhythms, unconstrained by the necessity to provide a steady foundation for dancing. "Bebop ignored the dancers," says Tito, and while many looked on this as a betrayal, others welcomed the excitement of the extended, adventurous solos and hot-peppered rhythmic improvisations.

The brilliant trumpeter **Dizzy Gillespie** helped originate and give status to the Cubop movement, a cross between bebop and Latin. While in Cab Calloway's band in the '30s, Dizzy sat beside Mario Bauzá, furthering his growing interest in Latin music. Dizzy founded his own band in the '40s; his famed big-band concert at Carnegie Hall on September 29, 1947, was a watershed in the Cubop movement.

Gillespie had recently retooled his band and also added **Chano Pozo**, a newly arrived Cuban conga player recommended by Mario

Feb. 7, 1947, Machito recording date featuring Chano Pozo and Arsenio Rodríguez.
Front row from left: Jorge Lopez, trumpet (Jorge was with Noro Morales for many years and played the trumpet solo on Tito's "Cuando te Vea" on Dance Mania 1); singers Tito Rodríguez and Olga Guillot; Mario Bauzá with side to camera; Gabriel Oller, owner of the Spanish Music Center (SMC) record label; Machito. Second row from left: Eugene Johnson, lead alto for Machito; René Hernández, piano and arranger; Chano Pozo, congas; Carlos Vidal, Machito's conga player; José Pin Madera, tenor sax and arranger; Arsenio Rodríguez; Miguelito Valdés, vocalist. Back row: unidentified man; Julio Andino, bass; José Mangual, bongos; Ubaldo Nieto, timbales and drumset; René Rodríguez, Arsenio's nephew.

Bauzá. Pozo belonged to the Cuban secret society called **Abakwá** which had origins in Nigeria. His raw, primal style brought a new energy to the band, and several of his compositions have become classics, including **"Tin Tin Deo,"** **"Manteca"** and **"Afro-Cuban Suite,"** which he wrote with Gillespie. Pozo stayed with the band until he was killed in a Harlem nightclub in 1948.

West Coast bandleader **Stan Kenton** also played an important role in the Cubop movement and the beginnings of the Latin-jazz style. Famous as the chief exponent of West Coast cool jazz, Kenton liked Latin music, too. Early in 1947, after playing opposite Machito at New York's Town Hall, he recorded a song called **"Machito."** He then disbanded his group and re-formed the band with even more emphasis on Latin music, adding Brazilian guitarist **Laurindo Almeida**. Later in 1947 he recorded his influential version of Moises Simon's classic, "The Peanut

Vendor," which included dissonant voicings in the trumpet parts and featured three percussionists from Machito's band, including Machito himself on maracas.

Machito and his bandleader, Mario Bauzá, also contributed to the Cubop movement. Record producer **Norman Granz** paired Machito and his Afro-Cubans with bebop saxophone genius **Charlie Parker** for several memorable recordings that proved a fruitful fusion of Cuban music and jazz. Machito's band also recorded or played with a Who's Who of jazz at the time, including saxophonists **Dexter Gordon, Zoot Sims, Stan Getz, Johnny Griffin, Brew Moore**, altoist **Lee Konitz** and trumpeter **Howard McGee**. "Afro-Cuban Jazz Suite," composed by Cuban trumpeter **Chico O'Farrill**, was recorded by Machito in 1951 with Charlie Parker on alto, **Flip Phillips** on tenor and **Buddy Rich** on drums.

Cubop soon became an established musical genre. **Club Cubop City** opened in New York with **"Symphony Sid" Torrin** as master of ceremonies. Sid later hosted an influential radio show called **"Jumping with Symphony Sid."** In the late '40s and '50s, jazz and Latin were both alive and well, living close to each other, and continuing to evolve and merge together.

Latin Influence on Rock 'n' Roll

Latin music strongly influenced the early American rock 'n' roll of the '50s and '60s, grafting Latin rhythmic elements onto blues and rhythm & blues material—Professor Longhair's 1950 recording "Mardi Gras in New Orleans," for example. Professor Longhair (Roy Byrd) described his style as "a mixture of rumba, mambo, and calypso."[9] Bo Diddley's 1955 hit, "Bo Diddley," introduced his trademark guitar groove borrowed directly from the 3-2 clave pattern. Bo's rhythm backup featured a clave-accented floor tom roll and the heavy use of maracas, played by the mysterious Jerome. The Coasters also had several Latin-influenced hits, including "Down in Mexico," "Searchin'," "Young Blood" and "Poison Ivy." Generally, drumset players imitated the basic conga tumbaó on the drumset by playing a backbeat on "2" and the small tom on "4" and the "and of 4," a rhythm used on countless early rock 'n' roll songs. Ray Charles' 1959 classic, "What'd I Say," featured a more sophisticated use of Latin rhythms—an up-tempo rumba pattern on the bell of the ride cymbal and the tom toms for the main groove, a clave-based tom tom accompaniment for the "ooo's" and "aaah's" in the breakdown.

Charangas and Típicas

The Cuban flutist **Fajardo**'s clean, uncluttered sound influenced many musicians when he played at the Waldorf Astoria and the Palladium in 1959. Fajardo's band featured master percussionists **Ulpanio Díaz** on timbales and **Tata Güines** on congas. Inspired by the older típica, or typical, sound of groups like **Orquesta Aragón**, pianist **Charlie Palmieri** formed his group **Charanga Duboney**. The group played its first performance on New Year's Eve, 1960. Charanga Duboney returned to the more traditional instrumentation of flutes and four violins instead of the more brash saxes and trumpets. One night when Palmieri was

playing in a club, he heard flute player **Johnny Pacheco** practicing in the kitchen. He introduced himself and soon added Pacheco to the band.

Mongo Santamaria came to the U.S. in 1950 with fellow conguero **Armando Peraza**, playing first with Perez Prado and Tito Puente. Mongo formed his own charanga, **La Sabrosa**, in 1961 with Cuban tenor saxophonist **José "Chombo" Silva**, a partnership that resulted in the classic 6/8 song, "**Afro-Blue**," later immortalized in a recording by **John Coltrane**. Mongo's music combined elements of Latin, R&B and jazz.

Another fast-paced dance craze, the **pachanga**, surfaced during this time but soon faded, some say because the dance was too exhausting.

1962 photo of Mongo Santamaria.

Brooklyn-born conguero **Ray Barretto** became a well-known figure on the New York Latin scene during this period. He had been part of the Harlem bebop movement in the '50s, jamming with players like **Roy Haynes, Max Roach, Sonny Stitt** and **Charlie Parker**. Barretto played on many recordings with such artists as **Lou Donaldson, Gene Ammons, Cannonball Adderley** and **Red Garland**. He started his own charanga in 1961. In 1967, after signing with Fania Records, Barretto began playing stronger conjunto material with R&B elements. His 1968 *Hard*

Hands album became one of his most popular.

The "Big Three," Tito Puente, Machito and Tito Rodríguez, continued to reign, but a new generation of Latin musicians including **Eddie Palmieri** and **Larry Harlow** began to make their influence felt. These younger musicians played a leaner, meaner, hard-hitting brand of Latin music based on the conjunto format— usually one trombone, two trumpets, flute, piano, timbales, congas, bongos and Ampeg baby bass (a fiberglass electric bass with an upright design, favored by the Latin players because it produced nicely sustained notes).

Pianist **Eddie Palmieri,** Charlie's younger brother, founded **Conjunto La Perfecta** in 1961. Machito's pianist, **René Hernández,** one of the greats of Afro-Cuban music, spent time as Palmieri's arranger. The band also featured trombonist **Barry Rogers,** later part of the original **Brecker Brothers** band **Dreams** (which also featured drummer **Billy Cobham**). Eddie Palmieri, who grew up in the Bronx and struggled with the difficulties of daily life in the inner city, made these experiences part of his music. As he celebrated his Puerto Rican heritage and encouraged others to do so, Palmieri combined Cuban musical tradition with **McCoy Tyner'**s modal jazz piano style into an intense and exciting avant-garde music.

Descargas and Latin Jazz

Cover of the reissue of Cachao's 1957 Cuban Jam Sessions recording.

The 1957 recording "**Cuban Jam Sessions**" (also called "**Descargas**"), featuring bassist Israel "Cachao" Lopez, master conguero Tata Güines and timbalero **Guillermo Barreto,** had a strong influence on New York's Latin musicians in the '60s. The term descargas, "discharge" or "unload," here meant jam sessions where musicians and vocalists "unloaded" their ideas, "stretched out," and developed longer solos utilizing jazz techniques in the Latin format.

Charlie Palmieri directed a series of descargas for **Alegre Records** which preserved the three-part Latin form, but extended the mambo section more than Machito and others had previously done. Similar jam sessions held Monday nights at the **Red Garter** and the **Village Gate** in New York gave birth to the **Fania All-Stars**, a loosely structured amalgamation of New York's finest Latin musicians, including Tito Puente, who recorded several influential albums with the All-Stars.

Boogaloo (Bugalú)

Puerto Ricans and blacks lived next to each other in Harlem and the Bronx and, naturally, listened to each others' music and combined forces. Some Latin bands incorporated elements of rhythm & blues in a new style known as boogaloo, usually played with the conjunto format which included trombones in the front line. Many of the songs had English lyrics with tongue-in-cheek, humorous themes. The boogaloo hits included **Joe Cuba**'s million-selling **"Bang Bang"** and **Pete Rodríguez'** **"I Like It Like That,"** and Mongo Santamaria's **"Watermelon Man."** Boogaloo turned out to be an interesting but short-lived style.

Bossa Nova and Samba

During the '60s, as musicians from other South American countries began to come to the U.S., American audiences heard the Samba and the Bossa Nova from Brazil. The Bossa Nova clave is similar to the 3:2 Son clave, but because the last note is on the "and of 3" instead of "3," the music has a very different, flowing feel. Saxophonist **Stan Getz** recorded *Jazz Samba* with guitarist **Charlie Byrd** in 1962, an album including the hit tune **"Desafinado,"** written by **Antonio Carlos Jobim.** On the follow-up album, Getz recorded **João Gilberto**'s Bossa Nova "The Girl From Ipanema," sung by Gilberto's wife, **Astrud.** **"The Girl From Ipanema"** soon became a standard played by every band, perhaps the biggest hit of many jazz adaptations of Sambas and Bossa Novas by these master Brazilian composers.

Brazilian percussionist **Airto Moreira** and his wife, vocalist **Flora Purim,** also became popular. Airto joined **Chick Corea's Return to Forever** playing the drumset, though he is mostly known as a percussionist. His quick and powerful drumset performances on **"500 Miles High"** and **"Spain,"** from 1987's *Light As A Feather* album, are considered classics in the Samba style. Airto later played percussion with **Miles Davis.**

The West Coast and Latin Rock

Meanwhile, Latin jazz was continuing to develop on the West Coast. Pianist **George Shearing** played a hybrid of Latin and small-group bebop with his band, which then included **Cal Tjader** on vibes and bongos, **Mongo** on congas, **Willie Bobo** on timbales and **Armando Peraza** on bongos. All these side men made significant contributions as

From left: Cal Tjader; Al McKibbon; Joe the waiter; Tito; standing, Miguelito Valdés; George Shearing; unidentified man.

leaders as well. **Cal Tjader** started recording on his own in 1954 with Mongo and brothers **Manuel** and **Carlos Duran** on piano and bass respectively; **Bayardo "Benny" Velarde** on timbales, bongos, and congas; **Edgard Rosales** and **Luis Miranda** on congas; and **Dick Collins, John Howell, Al Porcinio** and **Charlie Walp** on trumpets. In 1964 he recorded "**Soul Sauce**," based on Dizzy Gillespie's "**Guachi Guara**."

Latin rhythms had already been used in '50s rock 'n' roll, but in the '70s they became more fully incorporated in the styles of Latin rock and Funk. San Francisco's **Carlos Santana**, Latin rock's most famous star, recorded Willie Bobo's "**Evil Ways**" in 1970 and in 1971 a version of Tito Puente's cha cha chá, "**Oye Como Va**," that became a classic. He assured the authenticity of his sound by hiring seasoned Latin percussionists **Pete** and **Coke Escovedo**.* Santana introduced millions of white teenagers to the Latin sound and helped popularize the music around the world.

Oakland's **Tower of Power** blended the Latin rhythmic concept of ostinatos played by bass and drums and similar concepts pioneered by the **James Brown** band to create new and original Funk grooves based on the clave and other Latin bell patterns and accents.

Generally, Latin rock didn't impress Latins because it lacked authenticity, but this didn't stop virtually every rock band in the country from adding congas, cowbells and other Latin percussion instruments to their line-ups.

---

* Pete's daughter, Sheila E., has become one of the most respected percussionists in the world.

Salsa

I t's unclear exactly when and why people started calling Afro-Cuban music salsa. It may have come from **Cal Tjader's *Soul Sauce*** album cover, which featured a bottle of Louisiana hot sauce. What is clear is that after being named salsa, the music took on new life and popularity. Tito Puente insists the name was just a marketing ploy which repackaged the same mambos and cha cha chás he had been playing for 40 years, but the marketing strategy did work, and many artists including Tito, Eddie Palmieri, Larry Harlow, Ray Barretto, **Willie Colón** and **Típica '73** found themselves working more than ever.

The 1980s

B y the late '70s New York had lost its position as the center of the U.S. Latin music scene, and Miami and Los Angeles had become more prominent. **Gloria Estefan** and international vocal stars like **Julio Iglesias, Juan Carlos** and **Selena Quintanella** began to dominate the scene. Record companies released *salsa romántica* ballads with lush arrangements and began to tap the pan-Latin market. As in pop, vocalists, rather than musicians, became the focal point of the music.

Cuba in the '70s and '80s—Latin Jazz and Songo

B eing isolated from the U.S. and Europe since the 1959 revolution, and the subsequent trade and travel embargos, didn't stop the Cubans in Cuba from developing and perfecting their musical traditions. A new style of instrumental Latin jazz featuring electric and traditional instruments, Cuban rhythms and extended solos grew up in Cuba, soon taken by the best Cuban musicians to the jazz audience at international jazz festivals. The Cuban group **Irakere** achieved a high level of musicianship and came to the U.S. in 1979 playing their unique brand of high-energy Latin jazz to large audiences. Irakere trumpeter **Arturo**

Sandoval and saxophonist **Paquito d'Rivera** defected to the U.S. and continue to play concerts and festivals all over the world.

The Cuban infusion has meant a renewed interest in the stalwarts of the U.S. Latin-jazz field such as Tito Puente and Eddie Palmieri. California's **Concord Picante** label began to record Latin jazz with artists such as Tito Puente, Cal Tjader and **Poncho Sanchez**. Tito now has two groups, the **Tito Puente Orchestra** and the **Tito Puente Latin-Jazz Ensemble.**

In the '80s, Afro-Cuban music continued to evolve in Cuba in the form of **Songo**, created in the late '70s by bassist **Juan Formell** and drummer **José Luis Quintana (Changuito)** of the Cuban band **Los Van Van** (The

Go Go's). Changuito added a bass drum to his timbale setup, which he played while standing up, and the music featured new conga rhythms with more open tones. Other modern groups, such as **Giraldo Piloto's Klimax** and **NG LaBanda,** have added a drumset as well. The drumset player may also take over the function of the timbale player by adding a

Tito playing with Paquito d'Rivera, left. Johnny Rodríguez is at right playing the bongo bell.

set of timbales and cowbells to the left side of the drum kit. NG LaBanda's **"Echale Limon"** is considered the beginning of the new, heavy sound of Cuban salsa—**Timba**. Other popular Cuban groups which feature the timbales-bass drum combination are **Charanga Habanera, Charanga Forever** (with **Gilberto Moreaux** on timbales) and **Bamboleo.**

Afro-Cuban music continues to evolve, incorporating new elements from other styles, as it has over the years, while remaining true to its Cuban roots and traditions. The music that flowered in New York in the '50s and '60s is now a worldwide phenomenon whose influence has been deeply felt in jazz, rock and pop. New and exciting rhythms, fortunately, are still being created as the process continues, and new musicians explore new sounds and new frontiers.

Discography

Album Title	Release Date	Label/No.
1. Tito Puente & Friends	1950	Tropical 5138
2. Mambos*	1952	Tico 101-Vol.1
3. Mambos	1952	Tico 103
4. Mambos	1952	Tico 107
5. Mambos	1952	Tico 114
6. Mambos	1952	Tico 116
7. Tito Puente (and his Orchestra) King of the Mambo	1952	Tico 120
8. Tito Puente (and His Rhythm Quartet) At the Vibes	1952	Tico 124
9. Tito Puente King of the "Cha Cha Mambo"	1954	Tico 128
10. Cha Cha	1954	Tico 130
11. Mambos	1954	Tico 131
12. Cha Cha	1955	Tico 134
13. Puente In Percussion	1955	Tico 1011
14. Mamborama	1956	Tico 1001
15. Mambo With Me	1956	Tico 1003
16. Cha Cha For Lovers	1956	Tico 1005
17. Dance The Cha Cha Chá	1956	Tico 1010
18. Cha Cha At El Morocco	1956	Tico 1025
19. Cuban Carnival	1956	RCA 1251
20. Puente Goes Jazz	1956	RCA 1312
21. Mambo On Broadway	1956	RCA 1354
22. Let's Cha Cha With Puente	1956	RCA 1392
23. Night Beat	1957	RCA 1447
24. Mucho Puente	1957	RCA 1479
25. Be Mine Tonight, featuring Abbe Lane	1957	RCA 1554
26. Puente Swings Vicentico Sings**	1957	Tico 1049
27. Puente In Love	1957	Tico 1058
28. Woody Herman's Heat, Puente's Beat	1958	Everest 5010
29. Top Percussion	1958	RCA 1617

*Many of the records from 1952-54 were 10" LPs with 8 songs.
**Compiled from 78 rpm singles.

NIGHT BEAT · MUCHO PUENTE, PLUS

30. Dance Mania	1958	RCA 1692
31. Dancing Under Latin Skies	1959	RCA 1874
32. Mucho Cha Cha	1959	RCA 2113
33. Puente At Grossingers	1959	RCA 2187
34. Tambo	1960	RCA 2257
35. Pachanga In NY, with Rolando La Serie	1961	Gema 1145
36. Pachanga Con Puente	1961	Tico 1083
37. The Exciting Tito Puente In Hollywood*	1961	GNP 70
38. Vaya Puente	1962	Tico 1085
39. El Rey Bravo	1962	Tico 1086
40. Y Parece Bobo	1962	Alegre 842
41. Bossa Nova By Puente	1962	Roulette 25193
42. The Perfect Combination with Gilberto Monroig	1963	Alegre 853
43. More Dance Mania**	1963	RCA 7147
44. Tito Puente In Puerto Rico	1963	Tico 1088
45. Tito Puente Bailables	1963	Tico 1093
46. Excitante Ritmo De Tito Puente	1963	Tico 1106
47. The World Of Tito Puente	1963	Tico 1109
48. Mucho Mucho Puente	1964	Tico 1115
49. Mí Para Tí	1964	Tico 1116
50. The Best Of Gilberto Monroig & Tito Puente	1964	Tico 1117
51. My Fair Lady Goes Latin	1965	Roulette 25276
52. Puente Swings La Lupe	1965	Tico 1121
53. Tu Y Yo Tito Puente and La Lupe	1965	Tico 1125
54. Carnival In Harlem	1965	Tico 1127
55. En Su Momento, with Celio Gonzáles	60s	Teca LLS 555
56. Otro Descubrimiento de Tito Puente (with Noraida)	60s	Millie Latino 1050
57. Una Tarde De Julio: Fabrizzo and Tito Puente	60s	Rhino 501
58. Llamada de Amor: Tito Puente and Los Hispanos	60s	Musicor 3137
59. Cuba y Puerto Rico Son: featuring Celia Cruz	1966	Tico 1130
60. Homenaje A Rafael Hernández (with La Lupe)	1966	Tico 1131
61. Stop And Listen featuring Santos Colón	1967	Tico 1147
62. Brasilia Nueve	1967	Decca 74910

*Original title: Puente Now
**Also titled Dance Mania 2. Released in 1968 as The Golden Era of Tito Puente.

63. 20th Anniversary Of Tito Puente	1967	Tico 1151
64. El Rey Y Yo, with La Lupe	1967	Tico 1154
65. What Now My Love, featuring Shawn Elliot	1967	Tico 1156
66. Eras, featuring Manny Román	1967	Decca 4879
67. Invitation to Love, featuring Bobby Capó	1968	Misicor 4035
68. El Rey Tito Puente	1968	Tico 1172
69. Puente On The Bridge	1969	Tico 1191
70. Quimbo, Quimbumbia with Celia Cruz	1969	Tico 1193
71. Con Orgullo, Tito Puente and Sophy	1969	Tico 1198
72. El Fantástico, featuring El Lupo	1969	Cotique 1028
73. Etc., Etc., Etc., with Celia Cruz	1970	Tico 1207
74. Santitos featuring Santos Colón	1970	Fania 387
75. El Sol Brilla Para Todos, featuring La Lloroncita	1970	Tico 1206
76. Imágenes, featuring Santos Colón	1971	Tico 1213
77. Palante	1971	Tico 1214
78. Alma Con Alma, featuring Celia Cruz	1971	Tico 1221
79. Te Reto, featuring Sophy	1971	Tico 1222
80. La Bárbara Del Mundo Latino, featuring Noraida	1971	Tico 1223
81. Me Voy A Desquitar, featuring Noraida	1971	Tico 1226
82. Celia Cruz & Tito Puente In Spain	1971	Tico 1227
83. Pa' Los Rumberos	1972	Tico 1301
84. Algo Especial Para Recordar with Celia Cruz	1972	Tico 1304
85. The Many Moods Of Tito Puente	1972	RCA 3012
86. Menique, featuring Menique	1972	Cotique 1068
87. Tito Puente and Concert Orchestra	1973	Tico 1308
88. Revolving Bandstand*	1974	RCA 2299
89. Tito Puente Unlimited	1974	Tico 1322
90. The Legend (La Leyenda)	1978	Tico 1413
91. Homenaje A Beny (Moré) (1st Grammy Winner)	1978	Tico 1425
92. La Pareja: T.P. and La Lupe	1978	Tico 1430
93. Homenaje A Beny (Moré), Vol. 2	1979	Tico 1436
94. Dance Mania 80's	1980	Tico 1439
95. C'est Magnifique, with Azuquita	1981	Tico 1440

*Recorded 1960. Released as an LP, 1974. Released as a CD, 1993.

96. On Broadway (2nd Grammy Winner)	1983	Concord 207
97. El Rey	1984	Concord 250
98. Homenaje A Beny Moré, Vol. 3, with Celia Cruz	1985	Tico/Vaya 105
99. Mambo Diablo (3rd Grammy Winner)	1985	Concord 283
100. Sensación	1986	Concord 301
101. Un Poco Loco	1987	Concord 329
102. Salsa Meets Jazz	1988	Concord 354
103. Goza Mi Timbal (4th Grammy Winner)	1989	Concord 399
104. Tito Puente Presents Millie P.	1990	RMM 80375
105. The Mambo King (El Número Cien)*	1991	RMM 80680
106. Out Of This World	1991	Concord 448
107. Mambo Of The Times	1992	Concord 4499
108. Live At The Village Gate	1992	Tropijazz/RMM 80879
109. Royal T	1993	Concord 4553
110. Master Timbalero	1994	Concord 4594
111. In Session	1994	Tropijazz/RMM 81208
112. Tito's Idea	1995	Tropijazz/RMM 81571
113. Jazzin': Tito Puente & India (plus the Count Basie Orchestra)	1996	RMM 82032
114. Special Delivery: Tito Puente and Maynard Ferguson	1996	Concord CCD-4732
115. 50 Years Of Swing [Box Set]	1997	RMM 82050
116. Dancemania '99: Live at Birdland	1998	RMD-82270
117. Mambo Birdland (5th Grammy Winner)	1999	RMM 02828-40472
118. Masterpiece**	2000	RMM 84033

Masterpiece was recorded in 2000 and was the last album recorded by Tito Puente.

*Six albums previously listed by other discographers without dates near the end of Tito's discography are now listed in the '60s and '70s, making this album technically #105—not #100, as the title suggests.
** This was added to the discography after Tito's passing and was his last album.

Postscript

Hanging Out With Tito

When Tito Puente brought me into his garage in Tappan, NY, a few years ago, we were working together on several projects. Later, we were going to a video shoot for one of the projects. We needed to load up his timbales because he was going straight to a gig afterwards.

The garage was filled with instrument cases: fifteen to twenty sets of timbales, neatly stacked in their cases against the wall; trap drums; vibes, which he affectionately called his "venetian blinds"; marimbas; and piles of plaques, awards, keys to various cities, pictures of Tito with different Presidents, gold records, Grammys, rolled up posters of concerts and performances—in short, a lifetime's worth of musical memories.

The first thing that struck me was the old drumset gathering dust in a corner. "I played the drumset first," said Tito, "then I went over to the timbales."

Tito also studied the piano. He began the piano at age eight and he studied hard. When Tito was twelve he formed a dance team with his sister, Anna. They modeled themselves after Ginger Rogers and Fred Astaire, but percussion became his first love.

By age fifteen some were calling him El Nino Prodigo—The Child Prodigy. Eventually he became the most famous and influential timbalero in the world—El Rey de Timbal.

Tito was like an excited kid in a toy shop as he showed me the twenty sets of timbales in the garage—timbales painted in psychedelic colors, timbales painted in solid colors, timbales painted in day-glow colors, his six gold timbales, his timbalitos, his thunder drums, and the timbales that were originally painted with naked women. "They had to be painted over," he chuckled. "After all, I'm supposed to be a role model for a lot of people. You can't have that stuff on there."

Tito was a showman, as evidenced by the wild paint jobs on his many sets of timbales, his sequin jackets, his grimaces and tongue-biting during solos, and his over-the-head stick moves. He believed a big part of his job was to entertain people and make them dance, but he was also a very serious musician.

After a while we went into the house. Stacks of arrangements and yellow music-score paper surrounded the piano in his workroom.

As we looked over some of the charts, Tito tapped out the rhythms on the table top. "Clave—very important, those two little sticks," said Tito. "I always write the clave on the bottom of the score just in case the phone rings or something. That way, when I come back I know exactly where I am in relation to the clave."

He had no time for inferior musicianship, and if he found a mistake in my manuscript for this project or any of the musical exercises I had been working on, he let me know it in no uncertain terms.

I'm sure he was just as particular about how all the arrangements stacked in the corner were played by his musicians. Tito ran a tight ship, but he always expressed a deep love for the musicians in his band—"the boys," as he called them. Trumpeter Jimmy Frisaura was with him for forty years. When Puente's long-time bassist, Bobby Rodriguez, started to lose his eyesight, Tito bought an oversize Xerox machine so he could enlarge the parts.

It was time to go. Tito's wife, Margie, picked out his shirt and jacket and packed them in a hanging bag while we loaded the equipment into the trunk. Tito, at 76, carried his own timbales. I carried the stands. We headed to the video shoot. Tito drove.

We had lunch and then Tito got down to business as the cameras rolled. He talked about the history of "our Latin music," and he never failed to give credit to those who helped popularize it. He mentioned several people, adding a few kind words for each—Cachao, Miguelito Valdés, Mongo Santamaria, Charlie Palmieri, Count Basie, Xavier Cugat, Desi Arnaz(!), Duke Ellington, Cal Tjader. When the shoot ended, Tito was proud of the efficiency of his performance. "They call me 'one-take Tito,'" he laughed.

The first half of the day was over. Tito smiled, said goodbye, and went off with his "band boy" Ralph Barbarosa (who's been with him for thirty-two years) to rehearse and play a concert that night in Carnegie Hall! Just another gig for Tito. I wish I could have tagged along for that!

Tito died on June 1, 2000. A few months later, he was recognized at the first Latin Grammy Awards, winning for Best Traditional Tropical Performance for Mambo Birdland. Tito was the greatest—a real old-school gentleman and the most down-to-earth superstar I've ever met. He taught me a lot about drumming and even more about how to live life. We all miss him.

Jim Payne – NYC, July 2006

Endnotes

Tito Puente - King Of Latin Music

1 Sanabria, Bobby, and Ben Socolov. 1990. *Tito Puente: Long Live the King.* Hip: Highlights in Percussion for the Percussion Enthusiast 5 (Spring/Summer).

2 Roberts, John Storm. 1979. *The Latin Tinge: The Impact of Latin American Music on the United States.* New York: Oxford University Press.

3 Author's interview with Dr. Olavo Alen Rodríguez, Cuban musicologist, Havana, July 1999.

4 Loza, Steven. 1999. *Tito Puente and the Making of Latin Music.* Chicago: University of Illinois Press, p. 36.

5 Loza, ibid p. 33.

6 Loza, ibid p. 55.

7 Loza, ibid p. 56.

8 Salazar, Max. *Latin Beat Magazine*, Feb. 1994.

9 Loza, ibid p. 20.

10 Willie Rosario radio interview with Tito Rodriguez, 1967.

11 Hamill, Pete. *New York Daily News*, June 26, 1978.

12 Author's interview with TP, November, 1999.

13 Sanabria, Bobby, and Ben Socolov, ibid.

14 Loza, ibid p. 104, 120.

15 Hamill, ibid.

16 Author's interview with TP, November, 1999.

17 From "Salsa Already Existed," by Evelio M. Echemendeia, translated by Frank Figueroa in his *Encyclopedia of Latin American Music in New York,* 1994, Pillar Publications.

18 Sanabria and Socolov, ibid.

19 Author's interview with TP, November, 1999.

20 Loza, ibid p. 70.

21 Author's interview with TP, November, 1999.

22 *Latin NY*, April 16, 1973.

23 Loza, ibid p. 128.

24 *Latin Times*, April 1977.

A Brief History Of Afro-Cuban Music

1 Radio France. *Cuba - Les Danse des Dieux*, 1988 Harmonia Mundi. Album liner notes.
2 Gerard, Charley and Marty Sheller. 1998. *Salsa! The Rhythm of Latin Music.* Tempe, AZ: White Cliffs Media, Inc., p. 79.
3 Rodríguez, Dr. Olave Alen. 1998. *From Afrocuban Music to Salsa.* Berlin, Germany: Piranha Musik Produktion AG, p. 77.
4 Silverman, Chuck and José Luis Quintana ("Changuito"). 1999. *Changuito-A Master's Approach to Timbales.* Miami: Warner Bros. Publications, p. 15.
5 Roberts, John Storm. 1979. *The Latin Tinge: The Impact of Latin American Music on the United States.* New York: Oxford University Press, p. 87.
6 Roberts, ibid p. 87.
7 Roberts, ibid p. 101.
8 Gerard & Sheller, ibid p. 95.
9 Roberts, ibid p. 136.

Glossary

Abakuá - see abakwa.

Abakwa - or **abakuá**. Secret societies in Cuba which have their own sacred rhythms and rituals.

Baqueteo - Timbale style used in the Danzón in which all the playing is done with sticks on the heads of the drums incorporating muffled and open tones.

Batá drums - Double-headed drums used to call the gods or Orishas in the Santería rituals. There are three in a set: the iyá or mother drum, the itótele, the middle drum and the smallest, the okónkolo. They are considered sacred and are designed to reproduce the tonal changes and speech patterns of the Yoruba language.

Be-bop - Jazz style of the '50s and '60s featuring small quartets and quintets playing instrumental music with advanced harmonies and extended improvisational solos.

Bell - (Cowbell) When written on a chart, this indicates that the Timbale player should play the Mambo Bell.

"Blen-Blen-Blen" - Song written by Chano Pozo, Cuban percussionist and composer who worked with Dizzy Gillespie in the 1940s.

Bolero - A slow ballad, usually a love song with a tinge of sadness or lament.

Bongos - Two small, high-pitched, single-headed hand drums played between the legs while in a sitting position. The Bongos normally play a one-bar pattern consisting of a continuous stream of eighth notes called the Martillo. They are also free to improvise during the music.

Boogaloo or bugalú - Music applying a straight 8th note feel to r & b and jazz which previously had a swing feel. Latin music of the '60s and '70s, heavily influenced by straight 8th note r 'n' b.

Bossa Nova - A medium tempo Brazilian vocal and instrumental style featuring a steady Bass Drum pulse on the "and of 4" and "1," and the "and of 2" and "3," and a slightly different Clave. The 3:2 version of the Clave replaces the "3" in the second measure of the Afro-Cuban Clave with the "and of 3."

Botija - A clay jug which was blown into to produce low notes in the early Son and Changuí groups.

Bugalú - see Boogaloo.

Canciónes - Spanish songs featuring lyrics with guitar accompaniment which became one of the fundamental components of the Son style.

Canción trovadoresca - Troubador songs.

Cáscara - Cáscara means "shell" or "bark" and refers to playing the sides or shells of the Timbales with sticks. Cáscara also refers to the specific rhythm played. Both the style and rhythm are also referred to as Paila.

Catá - A mounted, hollowed-out piece of wood, struck with small sticks called palitos and used in a Rumba band to play the Cáscara rhythm.

Cha Cha Chá - Medium slow dance that evolved from the Nuevo Ritmo section of the Danzón. Credited to violinist Enrique Jorrín.

Changuí - Early predecessors of the Son groups, some of which still exist, using the original instrumentation of Guiro, Maracas, Bongos, Tres and Marimbula. Also used to describe the music they play.

Charanga - Originally Charanga Francesas (French orchestras) with the instrumentation: wooden flute, violins, string bass, güiro, and smaller tympani called timbales Criollos, or Creole tympani, which played the Danzón style. The term is also used for any group with this instrumentation, which can also include congas and piano.

Charanga Francesa - Literally "French orchestras" with the instrumentation: wooden flute, violins, string bass, güiro, and smaller tympani called timbales Criollos, or Creole tympani, which played the Danzón style.

Clave - The key, or fundamental rhythmic cell, to which all the rhythmic and melodic parts of Afro-Cuban music are related. The Clave is a specific, five-note rhythm played over two bars. Either bar can be played first resulting in 3:2 or 2:3 versions. There are two variations in 4/4 or cut time, Son Clave and Rumba Clave. There is also a 6/8 Clave.

Claves - Two wooden sticks which are struck against each other to play the Clave rhythm.

Columbia - A Rumba style based on a fast-paced, 6/8 rhythm in which a single male dancer challenges the lead quinto drummer to a rhythmic battle. The quinto is the smaller, higher-pitched lead drum of the group. Two male dancers can also challenge each other in Columbia.

Comparsa - Music and dance groups that perform in street gatherings and parades during Cuban Carnaval.

Conga also **Conga Habanera** - Cuban rhythm and dance performed by Comparsas (music and dance street gatherings and parades) during Carnaval.

Congas - Also called tumbadoras, these single-headed hand drums were of African origin and originally made from hollowed out logs with animal skins stretched over one open end. They now have metal hardware which facilitates tuning and are made with fiberglass or various kinds of wood staves glued together.

Conjunto - An instrumental configuration that developed in the 1940s from the Septetos consisting of tres, bass, bongos, three vocalists who played hand held percussion instruments (claves, maracas and güiro) and two to four trumpets. Congas and piano were added later.

Contradanse - French contradanse (literally "country dance") brought to Cuba by French colonists and former slaves who migrated to Cuba from the French colony of Haiti after the 1791 slave rebellion. Originally they were performed by orquestas típicas which included two violins, two clarinets, bass, cornet, trombone, güiro and "pailas Cubanas." The Contradanse evolved into the Danzón and the Nuevo Ritmo section of the Danzón developed into the Mambo and later, the Cha Cha Chá.

Contradanza - The Contradanse evolved into the Contradanza (Spanish spelling of Contrandanse) when the original instrumentation of piano, violins and flutes was augmented with clarinets, trumpets, güiro and tympani. The Contradanzas were usually played outdoors by groups called Orquestas Tipicas or "typical orchestras." Later they were played indoors for quieter, more sedate events by groups called Charangas, or Charanga Francesas (French orchestras) with the instrumentation: wooden flute, violins, string bass, güiro, and smaller tympani called timbales Criollos, or Creole tympani.

Coro/Pregon - A section of the arrangement during which the lead vocalist improvises and the chorus (coro) sings in a call and response fashion.

Cowbell - Originally an iron or steel bell fitted with a clapper and hung around the necks of cows to indicate their whereabouts. The clappers were taken out and the bell became a percussion instrument which was struck with a stick.

Cubop - A style of instrumental music pioneered by Dizzy Gillespie which combined Latin rhythms and bebop harmonies and melodies.

Danza- Musical style that evolved out of the Contradanza and preceeded the Danzón.

Danzón - One of the early dance forms of Cuban popular music. It has its roots in the French contradanza (literally "country dance") brought to Cuba by French colonists and former slaves who migrated to Cuba from the French colony of Haiti after the 1791 slave rebellion. Originally the contradanzas were performed by orquestas típicas which included two violins, two clarinets, bass, cornet, trombone, güiro and "pailas Cubanas." Later they were played by charangas with violins, wood flute, bass, güiro and timbales. Eventually piano and congas were added. In the Danzón all the playing was done on the heads of the timbales in a style known as baqueteo. An open vamp section called Nuevo Ritmo, which included elements of the Son, was added, and this eventually evolved into the Mambo and later the Cha Cha Chá.

Descarga - To "discharge" or "unload." Jam sessions popular in the '60s and '70s where musicians and vocalists "unloaded" their ideas and "stretched out," playing longer solos, utilizing jazz techniques in the Latin format.

Drumset - Percussion instrument consisting of bass drum, snare drum, various tom toms, suspended cymbals and foot operated hihat cymbals.

Ekué drum - A drum used by the abakuá societies in Cuba, which is rubbed with a thin rod to produce a low sound. The magic voice which comes out of the drum is then interpreted by a shaman or priest.

"Feeling music" - Love ballads of the '50s and '60s.

Funk - A syncopated style of Rhythm 'n' Blues based on 16th note rhythms and repeated bass and drum ostinatos.

Gallo - Literally, "rooster." Used to refer to the batá drum soloist in Santería rituals.

Gua Gua - A mounted, horizontal piece of bamboo played with sticks in Rumba groups. Used to play the Cáscara pattern.

Guaguancó - Originating in a Congalese fertility dance, guaguancó is one of the three styles of Rumba (Guaguancó, Yambu and Columbia) and features a challenge dance between a man and a woman in which the woman tries to avoid the sexual advances of the man. Played with tumbadoras (congas), cajones (wooden boxes), palitos (sticks), claves and shekerés.

Guajéo - The specific, repeated figuration for the tres (in the Septetos), strings (in the Charangas) or the piano player.

Guajira - Slower romantic songs featuring an idyllic view of the country side. "Guantanamera" is a prime example.

Güiro - A serrated gourd scraped with a stick. Previously, the name given to shekerés, hollow gourds with beads strung around the outside.

Habanera rhythm - The habanera rhythm, which was played on the Creole tympani or pailas, consisted of an 8th note, two 16ths, a 16th rest, two 16ths and a 16th rest.

Hembra - The larger, lower-pitched drum of the two timbales.

Hoe blade - The iron blade of a hoe which is normally attached to a pole and used to till the soil. The blades are used as percussion instruments and are struck with a large nail.

Itótele - The middle sized drum of the three batá drums used in Santería rituals.

Iyá - The largest of the three batá drums used in the Santería rituals. Also called the mother drum.

Latin-jazz - A style of instrumental music pioneered by Machito and Mario Bauzá which combined Latin rhythms and jazz harmonies.

Latin-rock - A style that developed in the '60s and '70s which combined Latin music and rock 'n' roll, emphasizing percussion and amplified guitar leads.

Macho - The smaller, higher-pitched drum of the two timbales.

Mambo - An up tempo style that developed in the 1940s and '50s from the Mambo section of the Danzón with elements of the Son and American jazz harmonies, including instrumental improvisation.

Mambo Section - 1. Open vamp section that evolved from the Nuevo Ritmo section of the Danzón. 2. Section of an arrangement, usually acting as an interlude between the Montuno sections, which features improvisation and new, arranged material for the horns.

Maracas - Percussion instrument originally made from dried gourds with seeds inside. The outside can be dried animal skin or

plastic filled with beads or seeds. They are shaken, one in each hand.

Marimbula - A box similar to an African thumb piano, only larger. Used to produce bass notes in the early Son and Changuí groups.

Martillo - Martillo literally means "hammer." It is a one-bar pattern consisting of a continuous stream of eighth notes normally played by the Bongos.

Montuno - 1. Open vamp section of an arrangement (repeated until cue), which includes the Coro/Pregón (call and response vocal section) and instrumental solos. 2. Also used to describe the repeated piano figure used in this section.

New Trova - '60s and '70s protest songs, using American pop harmonies.

Nuevo Ritmo - New section added to the Danzón which eventually became the Mambo and later the Cha Cha Chá.

Okónkolo - The smallest of the three batá drums used in Santería rituals.

Orisha - A god or diety in the Santería religion.

Pachanga - A fast-paced, energetic dance, featuring skipping and jumping, played by the Charangas in the '50s.

Paila - Playing on the sides of the Timbales with sticks. Also referred to as Cáscara.

Pailas Cubanas or Cuban timpani - The ancestors of the present-day Timbales, which resembled small timpani.

Palitos - Small sticks used to play the Cáscara rhythm on the Catá in Rumba bands.

Quinto - The highest-pitched of the three

congas used in Rumba. The lead drum which can solo throughout.

Rhumba - Used to describe Latin-sounding music which became popular in the US in the '40s and '50s. It included songs like "Begin the Beguine" played by bandleaders like Xavier Cugat.

Rock 'n' roll - Style of music developed in the '50s and '60s based on the blues and rhythm 'n' blues, and featuring a strong backbeat on the snare drum on 2 and 4. It can have a swing or straight 8th note feel.

Rumba - Rumba bands (not to be confused with the Rhumba, a commercial dance craze of the '40s and '50s) are percussion groups consisting of three or more Conga players, Claves and Gua Gua or Catá. The drummers sing while accompanying various dancers.

Salsa - Literally, "sauce." A term coined in the '60s to describe Latin music. It was not a new music but a marketing term used to describe styles such as the mambo and cha cha chá that were already in existence.

Samba - A medium to fast-paced Brazilian style featuring a steady Bass Drum pulse on the "and of 4" and "1," and the "and of 2" and "3," and syncopated Ride Cymbal and Snare Drum patterns.

Santería - The religion of the Bantu-speaking, Yoruba people of Africa, known in Cuba as Lucumis. Santería had a variety of rituals and festivities all based on certain rhythms and drums. Yorubans called their dieties Orishas and disguised them as Christian saints.

Sartenes - Frying pans which are used like cowbells and struck with spoons or other metal sticks in the Conga/Comparsa Carnaval styles.

Son - Perhaps the most influential of the early Afro-Cuban musical forms, the Son was a combination of the African percussion music of the slaves and the Spanish songs or canciones of the campesinos or peasants, which were played on stringed instruments. The early Sons (called Changui) were developed by the people in Oriente Province, in the eastern part of the island of Cuba, in the second half of the 19th century. The instruments used were the tres (a three-stringed guitar), the marimbula (a box similar to an African thumb piano, only larger, which was used for the bass notes), claves, güiro, maracas and bongos. In some cases the botija, a clay jug, was also used for bass sounds. This style is the basis of much of today's salsa.

Son Clave - Five note, two measure Clave rhythm used on the Son style. Either measure can be played first resulting in 3:2 Son Clave and 2:3 Son Clave.

Songo - A contemporary Cuban style which blends elements of Son, Rumba, and US Jazz and Funk and may include the Drumset in the rhythm section.

Son Montuno - Medium tempo Son-derived style.

Timba - A contemporary Cuban style which includes traditional and electronic instruments and in which the Timbale player usually adds a Bass Drum to his set up, which he plays while standing up. The Timbale player also usually plays the Clave rhythm on a Jam Block as part of his pattern.

Timbales - A set of two single-headed, tunable, metal drums mounted on a stand. They are played with sticks and also the fingers of the left hand. The timbales evolved from European tympani in late 19th and early 20th century Cuba. Cowbells, cymbals and wood blocks or Jam Blocks have since been added to the set up.

Timbales Criollos (Creole tympani)
- A smaller version of European tympani. Eventually these small tympani developed into the single-headed, open-bottomed Timbales of today.

Típico - Generally, "tipical," but usually meaning traditional, or "old style."

Típica - A band playing a more traditional or older, folkloric style.

Toques - Specific rhythms played on batá drums.

Tres - A small guitar with three sets of strings tuned in octaves.

Tumbadoras - see Congas.

Yambú - One of the the three main Rumba styles. The Yambú style, nearly extinct today, was originally played on candle and codfish packing crates called cajones. To add a higher pitched sound, players struck a bottle with a coin. It has a slow to medium tempo and is danced by male-female couples.

Bibliography

Bibliography and Source Material

Note: Much of the material for the biography section was gathered from interviews with Tito Puente. Following is a list of other helpful materials.

Alen Rodríguez, Dr. Olavo.1998. *From Afro-Cuban Music to Salsa.* Berlin: Piranha.

Figueroa, Frank M. 1994. *Encyclopedia of Latin American Music in New York.* St. Petersburg, Florida: Pillar Publications.

Gerard, Charlie, with Marty Sheller. 1998. *Salsa! The Rhythm of Latin Music.* Tempe, Arizona: White Cliffs Media Inc.

Hamill, Pete. *New York Daily News,* June 26, 1978.

Latin Times Magazine, April 1977.

Loza, Steven. 1999. *Tito Puente and the Making of Latin Music.* Chicago, Illinois: University of Illinois Press.

Noble, Gil. Interview, WABC-TV, 1999.

Puente, Tito, promotional biography courtesy Ralph Mercado, RMM Management, NYC.

Roberts, John Storm. 1979. *The Latin Tinge: The Impact of Latin American Music on the United States.* New York: Oxford University Press.

Roy, Maya. 1998. *Musiques Cubaines.* Cité de la Musique/Actes Sud.

Source material at the library of Harbor Conservatory for the Performing Arts, NYC.

Salazar, Max. *Latin Beat Magazine,* February 1994.

Salazar, Max, *Latin Times Magazine,* February 1977. Interview, "Tito Puente, the Living Legend."

Sanabria, Bobby, and Ben Socolov. 1990. *Tito Puente: Long Live the King.* Hip: Highlights in Percussion for the Percussion Enthusiast 5 (Spring/Summer).

General Bibliography

Goines, Lincoln and Robbie Ameen. 1990. *Afro-Cuban Grooves for Bass and Drums - Funkifying the Clave.* New York: Manhattan Music Publications.

Malabe, Frank and Bob Weiner. 1990. *Afro-Cuban Rhythms for Drumset.* New York: Manhattan Music Publications.

Mauleón, Rebecca. 1993. *Salsa Guidebook for Piano and Ensemble.* Petaluma, California: Sher Music Co.

Morales, Humberto and Henry Adler. i1954. *How to Play Latin American Rhythm Instruments.* New York: Belwin Mills Publishing Co.

Rendon, Victor. 1989. *Timbale Solo Transcriptions.* New York: VR Publications.

Uribe, Ed. 1996. *The Essence of Afro-Cuban Percussion and Drum Set.* Miami, Florida: Warner Bros. Publications.

Acknowledgements.

Jim gratefully acknowledges his teachers: Jim Strassburg, Sonny Igoe, Henry Adler, Eddie Locke, Chuck Brown, Philly Joe Jones, José Madera, Johnny Almendra, Adel González Gómez, Gilberto Moreaux, Blas Egues and José Eladio Amat.

Jim and Tito extend their thanks to:

Colbey Arden
Rafael Barbarosa (32 years with TP)
Louis Bauzó
Daniel Chatelain
Tony Clamenza
Martin Cohen/LP
Joe Conzo
Ina Dittke
Laurent Erdos
Michael Lydon
José Madera
Ellen Mandel
Ralph Mercado, RMM Management, NYC
Bruce Polin-Descarga.com
Tito Puente, Jr.
John Riley
Olavo Alen Rodríguez
Ramon Rodriguez
Bobby Sanabria
Paul Siegel
Brian Theobold
Ed Uribe
Rob Wallis

and especially thank their wives
Margie Puente and Joanna FitzPatrick Payne.

Index

DVD Chapters

Early Years
War Years & After
Palladium & Early Years as Bandleader
Birdland, Cu-bop & Latin Jazz
Vibraharp
Reording Hstory
Satana, "Oye Como Va" & New Percussionists
Tito Solos